SONG AT TWILIGHT

SONG
AT·TWILIGHT

by

Teresa Waugh

HAMISH HAMILTON

London

HAMISH HAMILTON LTD

Published by the Penguin Group
27 Wrights Lane, London w8 5TZ, England
Viking Penguin Inc, 40 West 23rd Street, New York, New York 10010, U.S.A.
Penguin Books Australia Ltd, Ringwood, Victoria, Australia
Penguin Books Canada Ltd, 2801 John Street, Markham, Ontario, Canada L3R 1B4.
Penguin Books (N.Z.) Ltd, 182–190 Wairau Road, Auckland 10, New Zealand

Penguin Books Ltd, Registered Offices: Harmondsworth, Middlesex, England

First published in Great Britain 1989 by
Hamish Hamilton Ltd

Copyright © 1989 by Teresa Waugh

Lyrics from 'Wait 'Til the Sun Shines, Nellie' reproduced by permission of
Redwood Music Ltd, 14 New Burlington Street, London W1X 2LR.

1 3 5 7 9 10 8 6 4 2

Cataloguing in Publication Data is available
from the British Library

ISBN 0–241–12825–0

Printed in Great Britain by
Richard Clay Ltd, Bungay, Suffolk

CHAPTER
1

Prudence by name and prudent by nature. I often wonder whether perhaps my name has contributed over the years to the shaping of my nature. Would I have been an entirely different person, leading an entirely different life, had my parents chosen to call me, for instance, Fleurette, or Diana? That is, of course, something which I shall never know, but when I consider my pusillanimous brother, Victor, I am forced to the conclusion that it is not, in the end, the name that counts.

My parents were yeomen farmers in the West Country. That is to say that the farm in Somerset on which I was brought up belonged to my mother who, as an only child, inherited it from her parents. She and my father, one of five sons of a local seedsman, were married shortly after his return from the First World War when both were young and eager to work the farm together.

They lived, I suppose, fairly happily despite having to put up with a certain amount of hardship, not least of which was the loss of several children. Of the six children which my poor mother bore my father, Victor and I were the only two to survive infancy. Pusillanimous Victor is four years younger than I.

Victor could never, from the earliest age, tolerate the discomforts of country life. When he was a little boy, the cold, the mud, the chilblains, the geese hissing at him across the farmyard, the rat scurrying in the granary, the stinging nettles behind the

1

milking-shed, the bats hung up in the barn and even the docile, brown-eyed gaze of the Jersey cows, all conspired to reduce him to tears.

It was hardly surprising then, when in his early teens and just as my father was looking forward to having a useful pair of hands to help him about the place, he announced that nothing on God's earth would persuade him to spend the rest of his life on a farm. My father suffered the blow stoically. Perhaps he thought, or at least hoped, in his heart of hearts, that Victor would change his mind. But Victor never did and when my father eventually died, my mother battled on alone for two or three years before giving up the unequal struggle and dying herself.

The farm was sold and the proceeds divided between Victor and myself, so that I was able to buy a comfortable, small house in the town where I worked for many years, teaching French in an undistinguished and little known girls' private school. At some time during the early seventies it was decided to amalgamate this school with an equally undistinguished boys' school in the same town so that for the last ten or so years of my working life, I was teaching in a co-educational school.

I am now retired. In fact I not only retired quite recently, but also moved house. I always planned to move, on retirement, nearer to where Victor and his wife live and so I sold the little town house which was my home for so many years and moved to a cottage in a village about seven miles away from Victor's more substantial establishment. This meant a move back to Somerset from the Home Counties.

My roots, as I have explained, are very much in the West of England and, quite apart from Victor's presence here, it has always been my intention to return to die where I was born, beneath the soft grey skies of the loveliest county in England.

Of course it is an added advantage being near to Victor. I have never been married and have no children, so when I speak of my 'family' I naturally refer to Victor, his peculiarly gloomy wife, Patricia, and their children. No one, I am sure, would deny that it is a great comfort, in old age, to live close to one's family.

I am very fond of my brother, which does not mean that I am

incapable of seeing what he is really like, and the sad truth is that apart from being somewhat pusillanimous as I have already mentioned, Victor is a pernickety, rather humourless and re-remarkably narrow-minded man. But he has been kind and loyal to me and, after all, we share the experience of our formative years. I say that I am very fond of Victor, and that is the absolute truth, but I sometimes wonder quite how much I like him. As I have explained, he is not a particularly likeable man, but he is a decent and an honourable one and I have no reason to quarrel with him.

As for Patricia, I do not really like her very much either. But then I imagine that few people do. Patricia, like Victor, is decent and honourable, but nobody on earth could pretend to enjoy her company. She is some years younger than Victor and must now, I suppose, be in her early fifties. But it is not middle-age which has made her so gloomy since she is no gloomier now than she was nearly thirty years ago when she and Victor were first married.

Patricia and Victor have two children, Leo and Laurel. Both Leo and Laurel were long awaited, or so it seemed at the time. I think that Leo must have been born about five years after his parents were married. Laurel is eight years younger than her brother. Gloomy Patricia yearned for children and would, so she says, have liked to have had a large family if it were not for the dreadful trouble she had in conceiving them.

It always amazed me at the time, and still does now when I think about it, that anyone with so despairing a view of life as Patricia should wish so ardently to inflict the pain of existence on others. But there you go — as they say nowadays. Leo and Laurel, when they finally appeared, may well have caused a fleeting smile to cross their mother's face, but it seems to me that from the moment of Leo's primal cry, Patricia has done nothing but wring her hands. Certainly, neither child has done anything to lessen their mother's nihilistic approach to life, and yet she must, I imagine, love her children.

It may well seem that I write this out of a sense of injustice and a feeling of jealousy because I myself have never had any children. I do not think this is the case.

Years ago I went through a very painful period of my life when I had to face up to the fact that, even if I did get married which seemed increasingly unlikely, the chances of my having a baby were slim. At one stage I longed to have children of my own, so much so that I could easily imagine the mental anguish which leads women like myself to abduct babies from outside supermarkets. But time passed and with the help of a basically stable temperament, I was able to weather the storm, accept my lot and devote such maternal feelings as I have to my pupils, to a certain extent to Leo and Laurel, and not least to Pansy, my most beloved black Pekinese. Pansy, alas, is old now and will not be with me for very much longer.

I shall miss Pansy dreadfully when she goes, but nowadays, as far as children are concerned, I can honestly say that when I consider the anxiety and the disappointment, not to mention the pain that so many parents suffer in these times of drugs and AIDS, and so forth, I sometimes wonder if I have not had a lucky escape.

It took a little while for me to find my ideal cottage, and when I did I was very nearly persuaded against buying it by Patricia who discovered a thousand and one things wrong with it. She was sure that I could never be happy with a thatched roof which was bound to harbour rats, with so open a fireplace which was bound to smoke, with the apple tree outside the kitchen window – one of the oldest and most beautiful apple trees I have ever seen – but which, according to Patricia, was so old that it would soon fall down, leaving the garden quite bare. She was sure that the cottage must be damp, the little sitting-room would never be big enough to house my furniture and the stairs were so steep that I would soon be too old to climb them.

Patricia put forward all these views with the best of possible intentions. She sees herself in life as the guardian of all wisdom, someone with a peculiar gift of insight. She, and only she, can warn us of the pitfalls which lie ahead, and it is her unquestionable duty to do so. No one else has her awareness, nor would it seem do they have the slightest understanding of, nor any ability to deal with, the most trivial everyday problem. It is so fortunate for us all that she is there to guide us. Yet when it comes to problems concerning her immediate family, however small or imaginary, Patricia collapses and is reduced to nothing.

The decision to buy the cottage was obviously an important one. I never wish to have to move house again. And for this reason I did, for once, listen with half an ear to Patricia. She might well have struck on the one fatal flaw which I, in my enthusiasm for this delightful cottage with its enchanting garden, might have overlooked, but I finally decided to ignore her objections and to take the plunge.

Patricia was appalled and full of foreboding. She is convinced that I shall soon be having to move again and that when I do I will have the greatest possible difficulty in finding a buyer for my cottage.

Victor, too, was rather nervous about the whole thing. Wouldn't I be happier nearer to them? It was, he thought, a lovely little house and the price was surprisingly reasonable, but I had been living in a town, and wouldn't I be frightened alone on the edge of a small village? Pansy could hardly count as a guard dog. I am not so sure. Pansy is not the least bit pusillanimous. Neither am I when I come to think about it.

I really enjoyed the move when the time came. It was invigorating and life-enhancing. The change was exciting. After all, I can barely count the years I have lived in the same house, doing the same job and meeting the same people day after day. Now, suddenly, everything is new, and how lucky I am, so late in life, to be able to have an entirely novel existence. Not only do I frequently meet new people, but the whole experience of learning to live not alone – which I have always done – but without the disciplines and routine of a job, is a demanding challenge.

I have, every morning, to find a reason for getting dressed. For getting out of bed. Indeed for continuing to exist. There are no longer little rows of children waiting to learn the *passé composé*, no more sixth formers puzzled by Camus's philosophy of the Absurd. No more homework to correct. No more lessons to prepare. Here am I alone. Prudence Fishbourne, retired teacher.

5

I have, I suppose, between fifteen and twenty years more to live. I could, of course, live for another thirty odd years, but I am not altogether sure that that would be entirely desirable.

So, as I have explained, I have no dependants, no job – nothing – just myself and a possible twenty odd years. Twenty odd years may not seem very long – but add to them yourself and nothing else and those years may seem like an eternity.

I have always been a practical, level-headed person and have always tried – not merely in the matter of my childlessness but throughout the tribulations of this life – to accept what has been my lot. To many outsiders my lot may not appear to be a particularly enviable one, but I have been, if not ecstatically happy, at least fairly contented. There have, of course, been highs and lows, disappointments and even the occasional brush with tragedy. But I think that most people of my age would have very much the same tale to tell.

I think that at this point I should describe my appearance – I have never been considered pretty but then I would never say that I was exactly plain, either – in fact, if you analyse my features, I should be quite nice looking. I am tall and thin with hair which used to be middling brown, but which has been white now for some years. I keep it quite short and I pin it away from my face, neatly behind my ears. My eyes are brown and large, my nose thin and bony, my face narrow, my eyebrows arched. My hands I have always secretly thought of as rather beautiful with long, tapering, sensitive fingers. My feet are on the large side. I would even admit to being somewhat flat-footed.

From the very beginning my main trouble has always been not my appearance so much as my manner, or perhaps my personality. I have never been able to achieve that lightness of touch, that delicacy of movement, the tilt of the head, the arch of the brows, the cheerful laugh, the frankness of gaze or whatever essential ingredient it is which ultimately attracts the opposite sex. I am perhaps a little too pedestrian, a little flat-footed in every way.

Now I am perfectly well aware that times have changed and that there are nowadays a great many young women who despise, or affect to despise, the male sex, and of course I entirely agree that men as a breed have a lot to answer for and that many of them are not worth the shoes they stand up in. I am also of the opinion that women are, on the whole, the finer sex, being in almost every way morally superior. Of course there are exceptions like Patricia. But, to return to the point, I have to say that, despite their self-centred arrogance and their emotional inadequacy, I like men and find them attractive and always have done. I do not like to find myself, as is often the danger with single women, surrounded only by my own sex. I like, when I enter a room, to hear a man's deep voice.

It is also worth remembering that although I have formed these opinions from observation throughout my life, as well as from the present climate of opinion, I was brought up in a generation which looked up to men. My father had been in the trenches and lived through the Somme and for that we, quite rightly, looked up to him as a hero. Never mind the men who caused that terrible war in the first place, we only thought of my father.

And of course in those days girls were expected to get married and they, too, usually expected to marry, so it was not without a melancholy sense of increasing disappointment that I gradually became aware of my apparently innate inability to produce that intangible something which would attract a husband to my side. Or perhaps I just never met Mr Right.

Only the other day I gave my name to an impertinent tradesman, that he might deliver some goods to my door.

"Miss Prudence Fishbourne," I said loudly and clearly over the telephone. "F.I.S.H.B.O.U.R.N.E."

"What a name to go to bed with!" came the reply.

I refrained from saying that no one ever has, since I regarded that as being no business of his.

To make up for this particular lack in my life, I have, over the years fallen in love with endless characters from fiction, starting with the obvious ones like Mr Rochester and Mr Darcy, and moving on to giants like Mitya Karamazov and Prince André.

Or sometimes I have fallen in love with the writers themselves so that Albert Camus and Molière may have found themselves vying for attention in my mind with Heathcliff or Henry Esmond. Such has been the substance of my dreams and these the frequent companions of my solitary hours. Surrounded by men like Heathcliff and Henry Esmond I suppose I could barely hope to find a real one who came anywhere near the required standard. And to be perfectly honest, I am quite sure that neither Albert Camus nor Mitya Karamazov would have given me a second thought had either of them ever met me. So there it is.

Despite this lack of a man in my life I have never really been lonely because I have always had a fairly large number of friends and acquaintances. The common room of a school is not a lonely place for among the mini-Hitlers and other misfits to be found there, one or two sympathetic characters are sure to lurk. In any case, the little Hitlers and misfits themselves provide company if one is desperate. But I have never really been one to seek company for company's sake. Perhaps partly because there is never any shortage of it in a school, whether one likes it or not.

In any case I have, over the years, managed to make a few true friends and in addition to them there is, of course, my family. So I have no good reason to complain of loneliness.

Nevertheless, I soon realised that without the school to fill my days and despite the fact that I am not only able, but happy, to spend large stretches of time alone, I would need to make new friends in the village where I now live. For one thing most of my friends no longer live nearby and although they come to visit me from time to time, one does need in life someone on whom one can drop in with impunity, someone to ring up when a storm has brought a tree down and the lights are out all over the village.

I am not especially shy but I do have, as I have said, this rather unprepossessing, pedestrian manner which means that people are not instantly drawn to me. At the same time, I am aware that a certain amount of excitement is engendered by the arrival of a newcomer in a quiet country village.

"Who," everyone will be asking each other, "has bought the Old Forge?"

And I know, of course, that their faces will fall when they hear that it is a retired school-mistress. They hope in their romantic, optimistic hearts to be told that Elizabeth Taylor's sister, or the mistress of someone on *EastEnders*, a criminal on the run, or Princess Margaret's butler — anybody, anybody but a retired school-teacher — has bought the Old Forge.

I must be bold, I tell myself. Go to church. In the parish church, at Mattins, I will not find Princess Margaret's butler, nor will I find many criminals on the run, but merely people like myself. Retired professional folk some of whom will be ready, I trust, to make friends with me, or at least to turn a kindly, enquiring glance in my direction.

So, when I arrived in the village, I went to church. I have to say that this was not an entirely cynical move. I have been a church-goer on and off throughout my life and have, if not a very strong faith, at least a desire to believe which at times becomes a firm conviction. Most of all I hate the certainty of disbelief and the pride that knows best.

Be that as it may, I went to church and there, as I had anticipated, I met, among others, the Postmistress, the Colonel and his lady, the Major and his lady, the Commander and his lady, and of course, the Vicar. I was politely invited to drinks, the Vicar came to call and within a short time I knew most of the village community, church-goers and others. They were all very polite and amiable, and all lived according to the roles in which they had cast themselves. None seemed particularly likely to become a close friend, but then it is not so much close friends as friendly neighbours which I seek.

On the other hand, I could say that my closest neighbour is not merely friendly, but almost too friendly. I suppose the poor old boy is lonely.

As soon as I moved in, Eric was at my front door introducing himself, pointing in the direction of his cottage just along the road — I had already noticed the immaculate neatness of his garden — and offering his services. How kind and considerate I thought he was. I invited him in and gave him a cup of tea and some home-made shortbread and the very next day he came round again to invite me back to his house for a glass of sherry and, he said, he would love to show me his garden. Was I interested in gardening? Of course he would be only too prepared to come round and give me a helping hand in my garden any time.

It was September and my garden had been somewhat neglected over the past few months while the house had been for sale and then while I was moving in. I glanced around at the late summer mess, a clump of straggling Michaelmas daisies in one corner, an ugly group of docks in another and a great bush rose — perhaps *Frühlingsgold* — spreading its arching stems in every direction, but almost swamped by head-high nettles all going to seed, and then I glanced back at the frail, bent figure in front of me. But, it occurred to me, he somehow manages his own garden.

"Well, that would be very kind indeed," I said brightly.

I don't think that I am a particularly irritable person nor do I think that I am unfriendly, but I do find that I treasure my privacy.

I can imagine that a newly widowed or divorced person may find living alone very difficult. It is something which they have to learn to do, but since I have lived alone all my adult life, I can no longer really imagine any other form of existence, and although I love company, I do not require it all the time.

Eric, who has been a widower for a couple of years, clearly does not understand this, as, after I had been for my glass of sherry with him, and admired his garden, he took to calling not just once a day, but sometimes as often as three times. I find it extremely difficult to be rude and have no idea how to discourage him without offending him as he doesn't appear to react to the merely gentle hint.

Ever since I met him, several months ago now, I have become accustomed to hearing the latch click on the garden gate and to glancing out of the window to see him shambling up the garden path, clasping a bunch of flowers, a basket of hazelnuts, an enormous marrow which it would take me a month of Sundays to consume alone, a Christmas pudding or a book which he thinks I absolutely must read.

Eric is becoming a problem. I do not want him in my house all the time although I have to admit to a certain liking for him and I would very much appreciate his company occasionally – but not every day.

Naturally Eric can hardly be expected to know that I am engaged in writing. I haven't told anybody about that yet, and it is, not surprisingly, very difficult to concentrate when one is permanently interrupted, and I find that I need to concentrate very carefully if I am to put things down honestly and, as far as is possible, from an objective point of view.

I do hope that in these first few pages I have managed to do just that and above all to give a true picture of myself as it has always been a matter of utmost importance to me to avoid self-deception of any kind. I flatter myself that, on the whole, I have managed all my life to see myself as I really am, and to see my motives for what they really are, and I sincerely hope that I shall be able to maintain a rigorous clarity of vision throughout the account which follows.

CHAPTER

2

It may be a truism to remark that in a school you see the world in microcosm, but truism or not, it is something which has struck me repeatedly and forcefully throughout my life. Even in the early days, when I worked in a single-sex school, there were the rulers and the ruled, the obedient and the rebellious, the warring factions, the sick, the needy, the strong, the weak, the generous and the greedy and, of course, as I have already mentioned, the little Hitlers. There were always plenty of those.

When Doble's, the girls' school in which I taught, joined with the neighbouring boys' school to become Blenkinsop's, none of that changed very much. There was simply added a rather unpleasing sexual element, an element which produced yet one more field of competition. Not that I believe competition to be by any means always bad, but I was distressed by the appalling spectacle of over-made-up teenagers vying for the attentions of the loudest, most swaggering boy in the school, and it was a tragedy to see sensible girls whom I had always considered to be quite pure becoming little tarts overnight.

Of course I am not so foolish as to suppose that those girls who look sensible, always act sensibly, nor do I suppose that their minds are always pure. After all, even I have had my dreams. But what I do maintain is that, generally speaking, a girl who looks sensible is a girl who in her heart of hearts wishes to be sensible. Just as everyone in the outside world dresses and behaves and speaks in such a way as to define the role which he or she wishes to play, so does the schoolchild. Only the role that the schoolchild chooses for him or herself is bound to change, sometimes with terrifying frequency before it is finally set, in young adulthood, almost never again to be diverged from.

Who knows to what extent the final choice of role is decided by environment or heredity, or a mixture of both? Who can tell, in the long run, what part free will plays in the whole thing? I like to think that it does play a part and that we are not all mere puppets of fate, whose destiny is decided by such arbitrary things as the name our parents choose to give us at birth.

In any case, over the years, I watched the children at Blenkinsop's grow and develop and flit from role to role as they floundered their way through what some people describe as the happiest days of their lives. Days in which insecurity breeds competition – often of quite the wrong sort – and competition of all kinds breeds yet more insecurity. Let me hasten to add that I am quite at a loss to know how any of this could be avoided since it is all, I am sure, quite simply a part of the human condition.

It is just that, as an onlooker, and to a certain extent I was not only an onlooker at Blenkinsop's but am also a mere onlooker in life itself, one becomes fascinated and horrified by all the role-playing, so that one develops at times a profound dislike for those who cast themselves as heroes and an almost painful sympathy for the unhappy misfits. The ones with walk-on parts which they have created for themselves out of some dark recess of their psyche, often provoke as much sympathy as the obviously tragic. It depends to what extent they are content to play that part. Sometimes they are dissatisfied with it and long for greater things. It is precisely here that I feel that I have myself come to terms with life, even succeeded in it. I have a walk-on part, a small part which I have to some extent shaped to suit myself and with which I am not unhappy.

Naturally it took me some years before I was able to mould my part as I wanted it and before I could really say that it suited me. I have heard of young actors and actresses who imagine themselves playing the great tragic roles but who eventually discover that their real talent lies in comedy. So children can have little idea which part will best suit them and some will have greater difficulty than others in finding one at all.

This was the case with Timothy Hooper. Funnily enough I well remember the day when Timothy first appeared at school. And I remember thinking, as I looked at him on that very day, that he was surely destined for one of life's walk-on parts.

It was about a week after the beginning of term – eight years ago now – and I was in the school secretary's office at the time, discussing arrangements for the French play which was to be on at the end of term. Letters had to be sent to parents encouraging them to support the effort.

Timothy was ushered into the secretary's office by his mother, a smart, remarkably young-looking woman who was, I thought, to say the least, over-dressed for the occasion.

"This," she said, pushing the child forward by the shoulder, "is Timothy. He's had chicken-pox. That's why he's come to school late. What shall I do with him?"

While the secretary made arrangements for someone to come and fetch the child and take him to see his dormitory, I looked at him. Poor little thing. He appeared frightened to death, small and frail and hesitant beside a glamorous, confident, pretty, impatient mother. It was as though she couldn't wait to be rid of him. Perhaps, I fondly thought, she is eager to return to some lover from whom she has been separated by the child's prolonged stay at home.

I have always thought and have sometimes been told that I should write novels, but lacking the necessary confidence, I have eventually decided instead to set down this account of Timothy's life at Blenkinsop's. Life is, after all, as they say, stranger than fiction.

Little Timothy who was then, I suppose, thirteen years old, had a face which could only be described as nondescript. He was also rather small for his age. I felt very sorry for the child, but, having a class to teach, I was unable to stand around any longer and so, with one last glance at the boy and his elegant mother

14

with her tiny waist and high-heeled shoes, I left the room and made my way down the corridor to confront the fourth form and the *passé simple*.

Some days later I heard from Timothy's form teacher that she was worried about the boy. He was very quiet indeed, even for a new boy.

Most of the children in the first year at Blenkinsop's arrived in the school having already been to school together and therefore knowing each other, but Timothy, whose parents had just returned from ten years in Jeddah, had been to school out there until now. That, combined with his coming late to a new school, was enough to make any child quiet, I thought. But I agreed that he did not look like the sort of child who might settle in and make friends quickly. I had noticed him occasionally over the preceding few days, wandering alone and disconsolate along the school's endless corridors, all of which smelt of boiled cabbage and disinfectant. He had dark circles under his eyes and usually looked as though he had been crying.

Once I stopped to ask him if he could find his way, and smiled at him in what I hoped was a kindly fashion. He muttered an inaudible reply and shuffled off down the passage, dragging his hand behind him along the wall.

I turned and watched him go just in time to see a large seventeen-year-old who was coming in the other direction with his spiky hair and his collar turned up and with the cockiest of cocky swaggers push him roughly over and say rudely,

"Out the way, squit."

I called the boy over to me and gave him a piece of my mind, but as is the way with cocky seventeen-year-olds, he lied his way out of the situation, swearing as he gazed sincerely into my eyes and, dare I say it, with an impudence that was almost sexual, that I had misheard him and that the whole incident had been a mistake. I glowered at the lout and walked away musing as I did so on the pungent smell of unwashed boy half drowned by the reek of cheap after-shave which had greeted me.

That year I did not teach Timothy's class and so any encounter which I had with him was purely accidental, but I did, for some reason – from curiosity perhaps, or compassion, or stifled maternal instincts – watch that child from a distance, enquiring occasionally from his teachers about his progress.

On the whole his teachers seemed to be quite pleased with him. He was not especially clever, but neither was he stupid. He tried hard and turned his work in on time.

I wondered how he fared on the rugby field. He looked to me like the sort of boy for whom the mere thought of a game of rugby on a frozen pitch might bring tears to the eyes and so I was quite surprised to be told that, although not naturally a sportsman, he was plucky enough and by no means a shirker. To my mind it was surprising that any but the toughest and the most insensitive of boys should care for rugby especially since I had learned by the grapevine that the rugby coach had a habit of running his hand inside the shorts of the younger boys to check that they weren't wearing underpants which were forbidden during sports for reasons which I shall never understand. I have sometimes thought that only women should become teachers. There are, of course, many bad women teachers but the behaviour of some of the more inadequate men who are drawn into the profession is nothing short of depraved.

But to return to Timothy, he apparently shone in one respect. He had a very beautiful treble voice and was soon co-opted into the choir where he sang like an angel.

During chapel I would sometimes glance at him singing in the choir stalls. Timothy looked at his best when he was singing, as is often the case with people who are doing something well, and concentrating on doing it. He stood with his shoulders back and his head up and sang with tremendous gusto.

After a while, perhaps during the second term of Timothy's first year, I noticed that he was often to be seen about with another boy. A fairly uninteresting looking child with the kind of face which is easily forgotten. But then Timothy, too, had a nondescript face. I was glad to think that the boy had made a friend and supposed that he had at last settled down and might even be quite happy at school. I could never quite explain why my interest in him remained so acute. Perhaps it was just because I felt so sorry for him when I saw him arrive on that first day.

*   *   *

I had been writing all morning and was quite engrossed with what I was doing when the telephone rang and I was surprised to discover that it was already after half past one. Gloomy Patricia was on the telephone inviting me to lunch on Sunday. Gloomy Patricia often asks me to lunch on Sunday. It is a day on which she feels that the solitary feel particularly lonely – and perhaps she is right. It is certainly kind of her to give me so much thought, but I rather wish that she could find a more tactful way of phrasing her invitation.

"I always think it must be dreadful to have no family on a Sunday," she began with this time. "No one to cook a joint *for*."

Leo, she said, would be back for the week-end, so it would be a real family party.

Leo, I have noticed, very rarely comes home for the week-end and I agreed, quite sincerely, that it would be a pleasure to see him.

"I'm not sure that Victor feels the same way," said gloomy Patricia. "Leo and Victor never seem to see eye to eye . . ." her voice trailed away. "I think there may be something wrong with Leo's attitude to work," she added thoughtfully.

It seemed to me that there wasn't much wrong with Leo's attitude to work, so much as with Victor's attitude to life. Leo was an actor by profession. He had spent three years at L.A.M.D.A. after leaving school and, like most people in his line of business, he was generally out of work. That hardly seemed to me to be his fault. While unemployed as an actor, he frequently took odd jobs in pubs or on building sites. In my opinion he had rather a healthy attitude to work, but there was no point in discussing the matter with Patricia, and even less so with Victor who abhorred the fact that his son had gone on the stage. He was permanently terrified lest Leo, a handsome young man with a mane of golden hair, be seduced by some predatory homosexual director. Anyway, I rather think that it never, ever crossed

17

Victor's mind that his son's taste did not perhaps draw him towards that conventional marriage which he, Victor, longed for.

Schoolmistresses, especially elderly unmarried ones, are notoriously narrow-minded people, easily shockable and incapable of understanding the modern world, and yet, I am permanently dismayed by the blindness and lack of understanding displayed by Patricia, not to mention the ludicrous narrow-mindedness of Victor. I cannot imagine what would happen if anyone ever dared so much as to hint to my brother that Leo's sexual leanings were not absolutely conventional and yet I would have thought that it was quite obvious that Leo is not what used to be called the 'marrying kind'. Neither do I think that Patricia has woken up to reality as far as her son is concerned.

I thanked her for asking me to lunch and put down the telephone with a feeling of relief that Leo would in fact be there because it would make a change and enliven the atmosphere. Besides, despite everything, I am fond of my nephew and have not seen him for a while. Laurel, his sister, I have my doubts about.

Hardly had I put down the telephone when Pansy started yapping to be let out, so I put her in the garden thinking as I did so that I would give myself some bread and cheese and an apple perhaps before taking her for a little walk. She is too old now to go far. Then I might return for a lie down. I usually like to lie down for a while in the afternoon.

I was sitting at my kitchen table peeling my apple — well, to be perfectly truthful, I had peeled it in one piece, as young girls do, and thrown the peel over my left shoulder and had just turned to see what letter it would form as it fell on the floor when the doorbell rang. I looked hastily and embarrassedly at the peel lying on the floor. It could be a 'Z', I thought, but then I know nobody whose name begins with 'Z', so I decided that it must be a back-to-front 'S'. Apple skins, I thought as I hurried to the door, always land in the shape of a 'Z' or an 'S'. It's a very silly game really.

And, of course the man to whom I opened the door had a name beginning with 'E'. He always did these days.

I was rather annoyed. I had spent the morning with Timothy

18

Hooper almost as if he had been really there and I was quite happy eating my lunch alone and playing childish games with my apple peel. I had no need of Eric just now.

Eric had a bunch of snowdrops in his hand, and a little sprig of catkins.

"The first sign of Spring," he said, stepping uninvited over the threshold. Pansy followed him, jumping excitedly at his calves. Pansy has grown very fond of Eric over the past few months.

"Do come in," I said. "Would you like a cup of coffee?"

Eric had come to call because he was worried about me. He hadn't seen me for a day or two and what with the cold weather, he wondered if I was all right.

I supposed I should be grateful for such concern. But I remained irritated.

"Shall I put these in water?" he asked indicating the snowdrops and busily opening the cupboard doors in search of a vase.

I felt a wave of such irritation that I wondered for a moment if I could refrain from being rude.

When Eric had put the snowdrops in water, he noticed that my coal bucket was empty and, without a word, he shuffled off through the back-door to the coal shed and came back a few moments later with it filled to the brim.

At that point I did feel grateful and somewhat ashamed of my initial feelings of unfriendliness.

"It's all in the day's work," he said.

As he sat drinking his coffee, Eric began to talk about his wife. He often talked about his wife. Sometimes he mentioned his only son who lived in Australia, but mostly he talked about his wife. In fact, I should say that she was his favourite topic of conversation. He didn't speak about her in a particularly personal fashion but commented more on her tastes, or remarked that she was brought up in Norfolk. On this occasion he told me that she was very good at arranging flowers. She always had flowers in the house. She believed that flowers in a house made for a calm atmosphere. My sense of shame deepened as he spoke and as I considered my own selfishness. Eric was, no doubt, a very lonely man and I should be glad to befriend him. Who, after all, am I to sit in my ivory tower making judgments on the world and contributing nothing?

Eric is kind to me, perhaps with an ulterior motive; but he is kind and he deserves my gratitude.

I began suddenly to take an interest in what he was saying about his wife. Perhaps, I thought, when I have finished writing about Timothy, I shall write a novel after all. And as he spoke I studied his face more carefully than I had ever done before. *Je l'ai dévisagé*, as they say in French. I took his face to pieces.

The funny thing is that up to that moment I had only really seen Eric as a sort of messy shape, recognising him by his gait and his untidy tweed jacket rather than by his features on which I had never before focused.

He might have been quite good-looking as a young man, I thought for the first time. He had a straight nose and good eyes, an altogether agreeable cast of feature. I wondered what his wife had been like.

"... she was a very good-natured person," he was saying, "never allowed herself to get flustered." He sighed deeply. "I never thought she'd be the first to go."

Eric sat there for some time, long into the afternoon. When he left I felt a sense of relief at having my house to myself again, but I supposed that I had alleviated his loneliness. I glanced at the snowdrops he had brought. They were delicate single ones. I fussed around the kitchen for a while, tidying up my lunch and the coffee cups, and wondered what to do next. I didn't feel like going back to my writing and neither did I really want to go for a walk. So I told Pansy that she would have to forgo her walk. Dear Pansy is so philosophical — she accepted her fate like an angel. Perhaps I would lie down, but for some reason I felt restless and uneasy. Eric had interrupted the tenor of my day. He really was quite an intrusive person.

*   *   *

I did not teach Timothy Hooper until he was in his second year at Blenkinsop's.

When he returned to school after those first summer holidays I was quite surprised by the change that had come over the boy. In only two months he had grown considerably taller, his voice had just begun to break and his pristine complexion was marred by acne, and yet he seemed rather better looking than before, or would have been had he managed to walk with a more self-confident air, with his shoulders back as they were when he sang in the choir. I wondered how he had spent the holidays and how his pretty little mother had entertained him.

For my own part I was glad to be back at school after the long holiday which I had mostly spent redecorating my kitchen, although I did stay for a week with Victor and Patricia and went for another week to Normandy with a woman friend of mine, a former maths teacher at Blenkinsop's.

I have to admit that I had a most peculiar feeling of expectation and mild excitement at the prospect of teaching Timothy's class. I felt, in some sort of way, as though I already had an understanding and a certain intimacy with the boy, although I wonder if at that stage he had any awareness at all of my own identity.

So it was with a certain feeling of trepidation that I entered that classroom for the first time that Autumn Term. There were nineteen children in the class and they were divided almost evenly into girls and boys. Some of the girls I had already taught at Doble's, but they had changed a great deal since then.

This was a class of fourteen-year-olds, and in it most of the girls were made up in a way that jarred extraordinarily with their school uniform, although I have observed that only very young schoolgirls make themselves up in that particularly ridiculous fashion. I wondered then at the adolescent male libido which was supposed to be provoked by so brash and yet so false a display of female charms.

Not that the young males were any more appealing. Except for Timothy. It seemed to me that although most of them were not exactly large, their bodies took up too much room. They spread their thighs in an aggressive, arrogant manner, pushed and pulled at each other like young puppies, and often smelt. They showed off to the girls who, in their turn, showed off to the boys and I wondered, as I often did in those days, how I was ever going to capture the attention of any one of them in order to instil in them the least understanding of the refinements of French grammar.

Timothy sat at the back of the class. He was quite quiet. The boy with whom I had seen him so often the year before was not there. He must have been in a different set. I wondered if they were still friends.

As the term progressed I found that Timothy, as other teachers had already told me, was attentive and reliable, but by no means brilliant. Although he was quiet, he was not unapproachably introverted so I do not know what it was about him that gave me a very strong impression of loneliness. Perhaps I even imagined it at that stage. I had, after all, developed a mild fascination for this boy and perhaps I invested him with feelings and thoughts which he did not have. In any case I felt a warm sympathy for him. So much so, that I found myself minding what he thought about me and hoping that he liked me.

We all want to be liked, but I have always attempted, in my professional capacity at least, to pay no attention to such matters. If a teacher is good at his or her job, and if he is fair, the chances are that his pupils will like him, but this liking should not be what he primarily seeks. I think that I can honestly say that although I have always been gratified as anyone would be by the slightest sign of being liked by my pupils, I have never, in all my years of teaching, gone out of my way to court popularity, except perhaps, very slightly, in the case of Timothy. I cannot say what precisely it was about him which provoked this interest unless it really was, as I have indicated, quite simply his forlorn little face on that first day when he arrived at Blenkinsop's.

I wanted him to know that I liked him and I wanted his respect and trust. I even think that I may have wanted a certain indefinable, but real understanding to develop between us; such an understanding as I fondly imagined a mother might have with her child. But by mid-December when school broke up, I had the feeling that, despite all this, I did not know Timothy any better than I had done at the beginning of September.

When school reassembled after Christmas for the Spring Term, I sensed even more acutely than before an aura of loneliness around the boy. Since his voice had broken he had left the choir and I wondered if he participated in any other school activities. I rather gathered that he did not and decided that if I could find an opportunity to speak to him alone, I might bring the subject up.

I noticed almost immediately that Timothy's work was not up to standard that term. He started to be late for lessons and no longer appeared to be paying very much attention in class. I wondered what trauma had come to disturb him over Christmas, or was his behaviour merely coming into line with that of most of his contemporaries — at least his male contemporaries. On the whole the laziest of my pupils were all boys. Perhaps Timothy thought at that stage that the role of the male teenager was one to adopt and that it would help him to fit in more easily with his peers.

I looked at Timothy sitting as usual at the back of the classroom. He was better looking than I had at first thought and he had an endearing quality of thoughtfulness about him. I imagined him to be a gentle, sensitive person. I wished I could help him.

About half way through that term, which was already going badly for Timothy, there occurred a very unpleasant incident. A poem with homosexual overtones, written on school paper in what was probably Timothy Hooper's handwriting, was found on the floor in his houseroom and pinned to the noticeboard by some well-wisher with, written underneath it in large, red, block capitals, the words 'Timothy Hooper is a poof'.

This disagreeable piece of information came to my ears from Timothy's housemaster.

So I took the opportunity to expound on my worries about the boy.

"The trouble with young Hooper," said his housemaster, "is that he hasn't understood the simple fact that school rules apply to him too."

I was rather surprised to hear this, as Timothy gave me the impression of being the kind of boy who, generally speaking, tries not to be conspicuous. And if you don't want to be conspicuous in an institution, you usually obey the rules.

"And the trouble with all you women," said the housemaster, "is that you're too soft-hearted. Let the little so-and-sos get away with murder."

Then he added something very peculiar. It was in fact so peculiar that I at first supposed that I had misheard him, but I thought about it afterwards long and hard, and I am quite certain that what he said was:

"You're all really just longing to be raped."

Even if I were longing to be raped, which I am not, I can hardly see what such a statement had to do with poor Timothy. If his housemaster was not prepared to take him seriously, someone else would have to. That someone else, I supposed, might just as well be me. I did, after all, have the boy's welfare at heart.

I decided that, at all costs, I must engineer a tête-à-tête with Timothy. In the event this was easy to do as when he failed to turn in his next two pieces of work, I had an excuse to ask him to come and see me.

It had been my practice over the years to invite various pupils for various reasons to tea in my house which was only some ten or twelve minutes' walk from the school and it was evident to me that my little kitchen often provided a welcome refuge for the chosen few from the hurly-burly of school.

So it was that I came to invite Timothy to tea for the first time.

CHAPTER
3

I wonder what has happened to Eric. I don't seem to have seen him for several days now. On Saturday morning I heard the latch click on the garden gate and I was sure that it must be he, but when I looked out of the window I saw the Colonel's wife from the other end of the village walking up my path. It turned out that she was collecting money for the village hall. I am permanently surprised by the amount of money which needs to be collected for various causes in this village. Since I have lived here, which is only for about five months, hardly a week has gone by without someone wanting money for something.

Anyway, Eric didn't put in an appearance all Saturday and I didn't see him yesterday either, although he may well have called while I was out at lunch. I went to lunch with Victor and Patricia, yesterday being Sunday.

Victor and Patricia live in a fairly substantial, very pleasant village house with a large garden and a paddock. They have lived there since their children were small and since Victor became a partner in the firm of travel agents in which he has worked since leaving school.

The house is sunny and, despite the gloomy nature of its owners, it is surprisingly welcoming with its wide sash windows and pleasant views down the hill and across the churchyard to the rolling countryside beyond the thirteenth-century tower.

I found Victor yesterday looking particularly pale and tense. He even looked a little mad, I thought, with his wispy remains of hair sticking out untidily behind his ears, his thin, drawn features and an almost haunted look behind his hooded eyes. But he welcomed me kindly as usual and handed me a generous glass of dry sherry.

"Leo," he said, hunching up his shoulders uncomfortably as an almost imperceptible shudder passed through his lank body, "worries me. He should have a proper job. His mother thinks he needs a girl-friend, but, as far as I can see, a proper job is much more important. He'll never get anywhere in life if he doesn't drop this acting lark. I have told him time and again that he'd do much better to give the whole thing up, come down here and try to get a job with one of the estate agents. Property's booming. It would make much more sense altogether."

I didn't think that Victor was really making very much sense himself and tried to put in an understanding word for Leo. But Victor is always very firmly set in his opinions and I doubt that he was even listening to me.

Leo, who was out of the room at the time of this conversation, and Laurel were both present for lunch. Leo was at his best, playing the part of a casual young man to perfection. Leo is clever and full of energy so that he throws himself into whatever he is doing with tremendous verve, and usually does it well.

Leo would not make a good estate agent but the role of an out-of-work actor suits him to a T. He has certainly managed at quite a young age to find what I feel sure will be his part for life. Perhaps it is made easier for him by the fact that he is not only clever, but handsome and funny as well. I may say that I find it quite impossible to imagine how he came by such qualities. His parents both appear to be completely nonplussed by him.

At lunch Victor and Patricia discussed their summer holiday.

Victor was in favour of the Lake District which might seem rather unadventurous for a travel agent, but Victor has lost his enthusiasm for leaving these shores since the Zeebrugge ferry disaster.

"You weren't exactly Marco Polo before," Leo remarked casually.

Leo was quite right.

Victor was just too young for the Second World War and later failed his army medical and so was exempted from National Service. The reasons for this failure were never really explained — to me at any rate — although I have the rather mean suspicion that enuresis may have been a factor. But then that is something about which I would never have dreamed of questioning my brother.

As a result Victor, unlike most of his contemporaries, never had an enforced spell abroad and I should imagine that he has only been there for pleasure two or three times in his life, unless you count Jersey. I seem to remember Victor and Patricia taking their children to the Channel Islands year after year.

It is, no doubt, peculiar that under these circumstances Victor should have chosen to make his living as a travel agent. Perhaps for him those journeys made in the imagination, undisturbed as they are by the inconveniences of reality — the lost travellers' cheques, the missed train, the disappointing weather — are enough in themselves, fulfilling and richly rewarding. I sometimes wonder.

Patricia, too, is very fond of the Lake District, but she would have liked to go abroad this year, just for a change. The weather is so depressing in England. Last year we barely saw the sun all summer. But, on the other hand, Patricia has no desire to fly. Aeroplanes, she says, are unnatural things. If God had intended us to fly . . . and so forth.

I sometimes wonder what Patricia has been thinking about all her life. Her endless ability to produce gloom-laden platitudes never ceases to amaze me.

Laurel, who is fat and rude and sulky and in her last year at school, looked sourly at her mother and said,

"Well, it looks like being the Lake District then, so you can count me out."

Victor wanted to know what other plans Laurel envisaged for herself and was filled with horror when she announced that she was planning to go hitch-hiking with friends on the Continent.

Patricia was in despair. There could be no question of Laurel doing anything of the sort. She would certainly be raped.

27

To set the cat among the pigeons, Leo, who was probably bored, pointed out that if God hadn't meant Laurel to hitch-hike. He wouldn't have given her thumbs. Some unfortunate people, he had heard, were occasionally born without them. At last he understood why.

Patricia scowled at her son and told him not to be silly. Wasn't he worried about his sister being raped? He might have something sensible to say instead of just making futile jokes. Rape was a dreadful thing.

"She'll be all right if she keeps her wits about her," said Leo.

Laurel, who is a born again Christian, said that keeping her wits about her had nothing at all to do with it. She knew that Jesus would be hitch-hiking with her and Jesus would never allow her to be raped.

Leo was comforted by his sister's faith but curious to know by what arcane process of elimination or peculiarly divine logic Jesus finally selected the victims of rape.

Laurel decided to sulk.

To introduce a happier note to the proceedings, I asked Leo what he had been getting up to in London and whether he had any exciting plans for the future.

Whatever else may be said about gloomy Patricia, she is an excellent cook, so that by the time we had eaten our roast beef, roast potatoes and Brussels sprouts followed by treacle tart and thick Jersey cream, everyone seemed to be in a mellower mood. Even Laurel looked as if she might be contemplating putting an end to her sulks.

The cheese was put on the table and although I could certainly eat no more, I was glad to see Leo help himself to a large slice of Cheddar. I always pretend not to notice that Leo has a habit of feeding Pansy under the table. Pansy loves cheese and Leo has a soft spot for Pansy for which I am grateful.

I did not stay long after lunch and wondered as I was driving home whether or not I would manage to get some writing done later, or if I was too tired. And then if I did manage to sit down and get out my pen, I supposed I would be interrupted by Eric. He was bound to call, I thought.

But as it turned out, Eric did not call which was rather a nuisance in a way, because had I been sure that he wasn't coming, I would certainly have done some writing, but, as it was, I merely frittered away the evening, watching television and doing the *Sunday Telegraph* crossword.

If Eric had come I would, of course, have offered him some supper, as I had a nice bit of cold ham in the fridge.

He may well not have come last night, but I don't doubt that he will be here today, just when I least need him so I will certainly not invite him to stay for a meal. For one thing I have nothing to give him now as I ate most of the ham last night myself and, apart from that, I have only a bit of stale cheese, not even a packet of soup to offer. Nothing else — no fruit, and no desire to go shopping.

It is bitterly cold outside, so I have built the fire up nicely and plan to stay inside in the warm. Pansy is curled up in her basket, obviously of the same opinion.

*   *   *

When the day dawned for Timothy to come to tea with me, I felt ridiculously nervous. I had a sort of feeling that perhaps he wouldn't turn up. He was obviously a shy boy and although he had agreed to come, he might easily think at the last minute that he wanted nothing to do with me. He might well have decided that my invitation represented an intrusion which to a certain extent of course, it did.

I had baked some biscuits the night before, and these I placed casually in an attractive tin on the edge of the kitchen table. I destroyed what I regarded as being the worst evidence of spinsterhood — that is to say that I purposefully left some books and a newspaper lying untidily on the dresser and a coat I left hanging over the back of a chair. Was I, I wondered, being a little foolish?

It seemed to me that I was not. I was about to entertain a shy and probably very unhappy boy. It was only natural that I should want to put him at his ease and how could a young boy be at his ease in a house which was meticulously tidy, reminding him, I supposed, of school and discipline? I wanted my house to feel like a home.

When I invited Timothy to tea I had murmured that I was worried about his work, but I had said that he might bring a friend. I had no intention of frightening the boy away although it is perfectly obvious that I could have discussed neither his work nor his state of mind in the presence of a third person.

I wondered whether, if he did come, he would bring the boy with whom I had seen him around during the previous year.

In the event, he came alone. He came nearly half an hour late, by which time, I have to admit, I was in a fever of anxiety, but he came alone.

When I eventually heard the front door bell ring I felt a quickening of the pulse. I caught my breath.

Why on earth, I wondered as I hurried to open the door, should I feel so acutely about this child. He was just another boy. Nothing to me. Probably just another lazy, rather dull boy.

I opened the door with what anyone would have described as a ridiculous grin on my face. I remember it now and I remember feeling tense and rather silly. My friends would have regarded that grin as being not only ridiculous but totally uncharacteristic. Luckily there was no one but Timothy to see me.

"Come in, come in . . . How nice to see you . . . I'm so glad you could come," I heard myself say in an animated voice as if I were receiving some elderly, illustrious visitor. I must try to relax. What on earth would the boy think of this dithering, middle-aged spinster?

All my nerves, I realised when I thought about it, were merely due to an over-anxious concern for this lonely, vulnerable, isolated boy. I had been thinking about him a great deal lately and no doubt all that thinking had just excited me. Once I had spoken to him I would feel altogether more relaxed. I only wanted this opportunity to gain his trust and to talk to him a little so as to see what he was really like – where his problems lay. There was nothing particularly odd about that. I felt sure that I could help him, if only he would let me.

Timothy stepped awkwardly into my house.

"Sorry I'm late," he said gauchely, shuffling his feet.

I ushered him into the kitchen, begged him sit down, offered him tea, coffee, biscuits, sugar, milk, bread, butter, jam, sorry no marmite, toast, gabbling nervously at what should have been a perfectly normal confrontation.

Somehow shy people have the ability to disconcert even the most self-possessed, making them speak foolishly and out of turn. In a minute Timothy would relax and we would be talking comfortably. Perhaps I should try, for a moment, to forget the role of mother which I didn't seem to be playing with any great aplomb, and revert to that of school-teacher.

By the time I had busied myself making tea and toast I had regained a certain amount of equanimity. Timothy, too, looked more at ease.

We talked about this and that, touching on the subject of whether he liked the school.

"Not much," he said gazing forlornly at the piece of buttered toast he held in his hand. "But it's probably no worse than any other."

"What about your house?" I dared to ask. "Do you get on with your housemaster?"

Suddenly he stared straight at me. Big, green, honest eyes.

"I hate him," he said. "He's a monster."

I have to admit that I was rather taken aback by the frankness and the sudden vehemence although not altogether surprised to know that that was how he felt. In my own opinion Timothy's housemaster was one of the most insensitive and uncouth of all the male teachers in the school. To be perfectly honest I had often wondered how he ever came to be put in charge of a house. Perhaps partly because of his wife who was a pleasant enough, apologetic sort of woman who would certainly be kinder to the boys than he would.

In addition to being an oafish bully where boys were concerned, this man had a dreadful reputation for ogling the girls and for being a past master of the *double entendre* so that no self-respecting girl could bear to be taught by him or to have

31

anything to do with him. He was the sort of small-minded, rather stupid, dissatisfied person who sees himself as a 'real man' and acts accordingly.

"He can be a little insensitive at times," I remarked hesitantly. I had to be very careful how I spoke to pupils about my colleagues.

"Did you know," Timothy asked, looking at me with his head slightly on one side and with the same green-eyed stare, "about the poem I wrote which they pinned on the notice-board?"

I was again amazed by the boy's frankness.

"Yes," I said, "I did. It was a beastly thing to happen and I'm very sorry."

"First of all," said Timothy, "I'm not a poof. I just write a lot of poetry. That was an experiment. Didn't Shakespeare write all his sonnets to boys?"

"Some people say he did," I agreed.

He couldn't explain that to anyone in his house so he just had to live with what had happened. Anyway it was best not to go on about it because the housemaster was as bad as most of the boys who thought that anyone who wrote poetry must be a 'poof' anyway. They were all horrible.

"Let's not talk about it any more," he said and averted his gaze.

I felt strangely relieved by Timothy's explanation, not that it mattered to me in the least if the child had homosexual tendencies, and glad that he had spoken to me. I also hoped ardently that he knew I believed him.

"Well, I believe you," I said as I got up to add some more water to the teapot. "Help yourself to another biscuit."

He did so and as he said, "Gosh, these are really delicious. Did you make them?" the tension in the room gave way to a feeling of more relaxed normality.

He stayed for quite a long time and we talked pleasantly of one thing and another. He didn't hate rugby although he couldn't imagine why as to be good at it you really had to be a thug. He had a friend – the boy I had seen about with him before – but they were neither in the same house nor the same form so they didn't manage to see very much of each other. I had the vague feeling that the friendship had never really got off the ground.

I asked him where he lived.

London. The holidays were usually boring.

No, he didn't have any brothers or sisters.

He mentioned his mother once or twice, casually, but not his father. I wondered if I dared probe any further on this first meeting. He had already abandoned the frank open gaze and reverted to his former, rather hang-dog, apologetic manner with his chin almost touching his chest.

I hadn't even broached the subject of work. I glanced at my watch. He would soon have to go if he was to be in time for evening prep.

The hour or so that he had been with me had passed extraordinarily quickly. He seemed to have only been there for a few minutes.

"I think," I said, "you will have to be going or you'll be late."

He got up awkwardly and stood in an ungainly way, staring at the floor.

"Look," I said suddenly and rather brusquely, "I did mean to talk to you about your work, but the time has flown. You must get down to it. You will put your mind to it, won't you? You should have handed something in to me yesterday."

"Yes, yes," he said. "I've done it. I mean . . . Well . . . that is, I haven't quite finished it . . ."

I couldn't bear to witness his confusion. I patted him on the shoulder.

"Come on, it's time to be off," I said.

At the door he turned, his head still on one side, a lock of red-gold hair flopping across his forehead, and I was treated to another of those frank green-eyed looks, and this time, a dazzling smile.

"The biscuits were delicious," he said. "Thanks." And away he went.

When he had gone I thought: there is something quite extraordinary about that boy.

The something had to do with honesty. I felt that Timothy

33

was basically an honest person. By which I do not mean that he was incapable of telling a lie. No child has ever been born who was incapable of telling a lie and it has always seemed to me that children have far more reason for lying than adults. Unless they lie occasionally they are in danger of being stripped of all privacy by the grown-up world which surrounds them.

When Timothy had left and as I tidied away the tea things, I went over every detail of our conversation in my mind. I wondered, too, why he had come for what could have amounted merely to a confrontation about his work. It was quite brave in a way to come, and to come all alone. I was reconfirmed in my awareness of his loneliness. But I also thought, with a certain amount of gratification, that he must have quite liked me.

He certainly liked my biscuits, I thought with smug satisfaction as I tidied away the box. I picked up the coat which I had left lying so messily over a chair and hung that where it belonged. I must be getting silly, I thought with a wry smile to myself.

I hoped, as I finally sat down to correct a mountain of papers, that Timothy might make a habit of coming to tea with me. Perhaps I would be able to help him with his problems, not that I was yet sure what they were. But he certainly had them.

It took me hours to mark those papers that night. I seem to remember that my mind kept on and on returning to Timothy.

*   *   *

It is now Thursday and I think that nearly a week had gone by without my having seen Eric when he turned up this morning.

I suppose I should really have gone to call on him and I cannot think why I didn't. I spent Monday writing, on Tuesday I went shopping in our local town and yesterday I had a visit from an old friend who came for lunch and stayed for most of the afternoon. I was pleased to see her and to catch up with her news. So what with one thing and another I have been quite busy and the week has flown by.

"Eric," I said as I opened the door to him this morning, "What have you been up to? I haven't seen you for days. Come in and have some coffee."

He looked rather grey and even frailer than before as he shambled into the kitchen. His clothing was messier than usual, thrown onto his skinny body in the most haphazard of fashions. Why is it, I wondered with a certain amount of distaste, that old men seem, with monotonous regularity, to forget to do up their fly-buttons? Or perhaps they just can't be bothered.

'Bitterly cold, isn't it?' said Eric rubbing his hands together and hunching up his scrawny shoulders.

"What have you been up to then, this past week?" I asked as I put the coffee on the table.

The poor man had been in bed with bronchitis. The doctor had called a couple of times, put him on antibiotics and told him to keep warm.

I felt very ashamed. If I had been in bed for a week, Eric would have been doing my shopping, making me soup, bringing me flowers and, for all I know, sitting by my bed reading out loud to me.

"Oh Eric," I said lamely, "you should have given me a ring, I could have come in to look after you. Or if you wanted anything from the shops I could have got it for you."

"Nothing to worry about," he said. "I just kept warm, stayed in out of the cold. I'm much better now."

"You don't look it," I heard myself remark tartly.

He smiled wanly into his coffee cup, and I decided that the least I could do was to offer the poor man some lunch. I wondered if anyone had been in to see him during the whole week.

CHAPTER
4

March 18th

We have been having a lovely spell of early Spring sunshine for the past few days, so that I have rather abandoned my writing and have spent most of the time tidying up my garden or taking Pansy for little walks.

Yesterday morning I was in the garden when Eric came by. He was quite elated by the sunshine. It made one want to get out and about, he said, and then, to my surprise, asked me if I would like to go for a drive with him that afternoon. He fancied a trip across country to Porlock and Lynton. We might stop for a stroll on Exmoor. Pansy would probably enjoy that.

To tell the truth I was delighted. My back was beginning to ache from gardening and it is many, many years since I last went to Porlock, so I found the idea quite enticing. Besides, I warmed to the cheerful, almost animated expression on Eric's frequently all too lugubrious face.

We had a delightful afternoon. The wide, clear sky above Exmoor was cloudless, the air was bright and clean and when we reached Porlock the sea sparkled as blue as the Mediterranean.

When we returned home in the early evening I realised that I had not been irritated by Eric once during the whole afternoon. The fact that he had made himself look quite tidy for a change and even managed to do up his fly-buttons may well have contributed towards my feelings of good will.

But, I have to admit that beyond that he was companionable and pleasant. Besides which Eric has the most exquisite, old-fashioned good manners. He is the sort of man who will always walk on the outside if he is accompanying a woman along a pavement – and good manners, of course, never fail to please.

We came home via Minehead where we stopped in a dingy little café for a cup of watery tea and a couple of stale biscuits, but we had had a good time so I was not displeased when Eric suggested that we should go on more such outings. He had lived in Somerset only since his retirement, four years earlier, but he was remarkably unfamiliar with the county and loath to go sightseeing alone.

Next week, if the weather is fine, we are thinking of making a day of it and going to Wells.

I was mildly surprised to learn that Eric had only lived in Somerset for so short a time and surprised, too, to realise that despite the frequency of our meetings over the past months, I know very little about him. I don't know where he has spent most of his life, nor indeed do I really have any idea how he has spent it. All I seem to know is that his wife loved flowers and was a good cook. I wonder if I have been very remiss in not asking him about his life, or if he is just someone who does not naturally talk about himself. The more I think about it, the more I realise that his conversation is rarely at all personal.

When we go to Wells I shall make a point of asking him a few questions. Perhaps he even longs for someone who will take a genuine interest in him.

*   *   *

As time progressed Timothy became a more and more frequent visitor to my house. To begin with he used to drop in for tea, perhaps once a week, but then he started to come even more often. Sometimes he would look in during a free period in the hopes of finding me at home, so that in fact, it was not long before we began to have a pretty clear picture of each other's timetables. He had, for instance, two free periods between break and lunch on a Tuesday morning which coincided with my not teaching.

37

To begin with Timothy did not turn up every Tuesday morning, but towards the end of the term when he had begun to come more regularly, I noticed that if he wasn't there by half past eleven I would be anxiously looking at my watch and wondering whether or not I dared to go out. It would be a shame to go and leave the poor boy to find the house empty, even though I would be seeing him again on Thursday, the day on which he always came to tea. It was obvious to me that if he came, he came in search of something and the last thing I wanted to do was to let him down.

I had grown quite fond of Timothy and although, never having had any children, I cannot speak with authority on the matter, I assume that the affection I felt for him was not far removed from what I might have felt for a son of my own.

What he felt for me I could not tell although I spent hours and hours wondering. I worried whether or not I was a disturbing influence on him. By providing some sort of a second home or at least an escape from school, was I perhaps encouraging him to cut himself off from his peers, not to participate fully in school life? I thought not, on the whole. And at least the standard of his work had marginally improved during the term, which was in itself a good thing.

Timothy, I was sure, needed me. He had, I gathered, a more or less unsatisfactory home life and what was more natural under the circumstances than that he should come to look on a well-disposed middle-aged woman as a substitute mother figure? If I could help or comfort him in any way, nothing could make me happier. I had of course to be careful not to allow my concern for him to interfere with the normal course of my work. There was no real reason why it should, except that I did notice that I spent an inordinate amount of time thinking about the child.

When he was late for tea, I worried lest he had had an accident, or sometimes it occurred to me that I might have offended him and that he no longer wished to see me. When he said good-bye on Thursday evenings, in time to return to school for prep, I found myself idiotically counting the days until Tuesday. Since I taught Timothy French every day of the week, except Sunday, I really cannot imagine why I was so anxious. It was, or so it seemed to me at the time, as though I had a terrible haunting fear that something awful might happen to him if I didn't watch over him; and almost as great a dread that he might reject me, as children have been known to do to their parents.

I began to realise the agony that some mothers must suffer over their children. Yet, for all the anxiety, I would not for the world have been without Timothy. My affection for him had brought an added intensity and excitement to my life which I would have been more than reluctant to forego.

All I could hope was that in some way I might bring something to him in return.

On the last Thursday of term I was expecting Timothy to tea as usual. I was half looking forward to his coming and half saddened by the awareness that I would not be seeing him again for four weeks over the Christmas break.

I had made a special cake as a concession to the Christmas season and was ready for tea at least half an hour before Timothy was due. Toasted, buttered crumpets were being kept warm in the oven. I hoped they would not dry out.

For some reason I felt hot and flustered and inexplicably nervous. Perhaps if I went upstairs and brushed my hair and powered my nose, I might feel a little calmer. It had been a long term. The Autumn Term was always the most trying so I suppose that what I really needed was a well-earned rest.

I peered at my face in my bedroom looking-glass. I was in my mid-fifties at the time – seven years have passed since then – and my hair was not white as it is now. I had always thought that I bore my years well and that, as is often the case with spinsters and childless women, I had retained a certain youthful vigour. Suddenly I looked a hundred years old. Timothy's mother, I realised, was probably young enough to be my daughter. To Timothy I probably seemed like a very old woman.

A surge of panic welled up inside me. What on earth did that matter? Of course Timothy could see exactly how old I was – to within a year or two. And what did Timothy's opinion of my age have to do with anything so long as he liked the cake and the buttered crumpets?

I brushed my hair neatly and put on a little lipstick. My face looked grey, there were bags under my eyes and the skin under my chin was beginning to sag noticeably. I dabbed some lavender water behind each ear and decided to change my fawn shirt and brown cardigan for a new, raspberry pink jersey which I had bought only a few days earlier. In fact I hadn't yet worn it as I had half a mind to give it to Patricia for Christmas. But I definitely needed brightening up so I put it on. I would find something else for Patricia.

My nerves were hardly any calmer by the time Timothy turned up, but when I saw his eyes brighten at the sight of the cake, I relaxed a little.

Apart from being pleased by the cake and the crumpets, Timothy was a little on the glum side. He was not looking forward to the Christmas holidays at all.

I knew from our former conversations that Timothy's parents were in the process of divorcing. He didn't talk much about the divorce, but it was clear that his father had 'another woman' to whom Timothy occasionally referred with a sneer as 'her' or 'she'. As for his mother, he said nothing about her private life, but merely complained about the smallness of the mews house into which she was moving. The approach of the holidays seemed to have cast him into a terrible gloom.

What, I wondered, could be done to help him.

"I hate Christmas," Timothy said with venom as he helped himself to a third crumpet. He had long tapering fingers. Like mine, I thought.

It was sad, I felt, to hear a child saying that he hated Christmas.

"Perhaps your mother will have arranged something nice for you," I said brightly.

Christmas Day itself would be spent with his grand-parents in Hampstead. They were all right, but terribly boring. There would be nothing to do for the rest of the holidays but hang around.

I felt disconsolate. It was a shame that a boy who didn't like school should feel even more negative about home.

Suddenly I had a bright idea. Leo, who was then eighteen and had just started acting school, would certainly not be spending the entire holidays with his parents. Of that I was sure.

Leo was a kind and amusing boy and I would introduce him to Timothy. Of course Timothy was much younger than Leo, but I didn't see why that should prevent Leo from being occasionally kind to him. I would go to London next week and arrange for the two to meet.

Joan, one of my oldest friends, lives in London. She was widowed some years ago and although her two children have left home, she still lives in a substantial house in Putney. She and I were at school together and have never lost touch throughout the years. Whenever I go to London, I stay with her in Putney and am always made to feel welcome. She would not in the least bit mind if I asked Leo and Timothy to supper one night. I decided to invite myself to stay for a couple of days before going on down to Somerset for Christmas which I planned to spend, as usual, with Victor and Patricia. I could finish my Christmas shopping in London and perhaps go to the theatre with Joan.

I was thrilled with the idea. It would give me a chance, apart from anything else, to check that Timothy was going to be all right during the holidays.

With my new plan afoot I began to look forward to the holidays, not just for the break but because I was looking forward to my jaunt to London.

When I told Timothy of my plan he seemed delighted, perhaps not so much by the idea of seeing an elderly school mistress during the holidays as by the lure of an older, grown-up young man at acting school. He gave me his address — a very smart one, I thought, in South Kensington — and telephone number and I promised to ring him as soon as I got to London.

Despite these plans I felt a foolish constriction of the heart as we said good-bye and a somewhat unsuitable urge to put my arms around him and give him a kiss. He looked so forlorn standing there, so lanky and so *distrait.*

When I reached London, Joan and I gave a great deal of thought to our menu for the evening. She sadly missed the company of young people since her children had gone away and so was quite happy at the prospect of entertaining Leo and Timothy.

Leo, when I telephoned him, accepted with alacrity. I rather suspect that he was more tempted by the prospect of a square meal than by the idea of spending an evening with his spinster aunt and her middle-aged friend.

But he would have been surprised had he seen his spinster aunt and her middle-aged friend preparing the supper. We had done the shopping the day before and managed to spend almost the entire day in the kitchen, giggling and joking like two schoolgirls. It seemed impossible that so simple a plan as ours for the evening could engender such childlike high spirits and so much excitement.

I have to admit that I was more than curious to see what Timothy would be like away from the environment of school, and not a little nervous lest the flow of conversation should dry up and there be awkward silences. I just hoped that Leo would keep the ball rolling. He is a naturally talkative and ebullient sort of person — not to say something of a show-off.

By the time everything was ready for the boys, Joan and I were fairly exhausted. The table was laid. We had bought a pâté for first course. It looked quite inviting on a large green plate surrounded by olives and gherkins. There was white bread and brown and pitta bread; the enormous chicken, stuffed with ham and onions and celery, was cooking away in the oven. The potatoes were mashed, the carrots and Brussels sprouts ready and keeping warm, and the jam roly-poly steaming gently on the hob. There was cream in a jug and the coffee was made so that it only needed to be heated up. We hoped there was enough to eat. Boys have such dreadfully large appetites. But then there were cheese and biscuits to fill the gaps at the end if they were still hungry.

For my part I had begun to feel nervous and knew that I would hardly want to eat any of it. I needed to go and have a wash and change and to get rid of the smell of cooking which seemed to be clinging to my hair and clothes.

I put on a light green dress which had always been a favourite of mine as I felt it gave me a softer, more feminine look, making me, I hoped, a little less school-mistressy, and a pair of nice black court shoes. I fastened my jade beads around my neck, thinking as I did so, that one should always try to look one's best, whatever one's age, as much as anything for reasons of good manners. The boys would certainly have made themselves tidy. So indeed should we.

Timothy arrived first, very punctually. The door bell rang shrilly, causing my heart to pound unexpectedly.

'You go,' said Joan.

I hurried down the passage to the door, my high heels tapping emphatically on the Marley tiles. Through the dappled glass pane on the front door I could discern the shape of a head, but could not tell if it was Leo's or Timothy's.

When I opened the door and saw Timothy standing there with a quizzical expression on his face as though he wondered if he had come to the right house, I again felt the urge to kiss him. But then I decided against it. He might not like it and besides, I had to remember that before very long we would be back in the world of school. I had to remember, too, that I was not Timothy's mother, nor even his aunt, but his French teacher.

Timothy looked delightfully fresh and clean and was wearing a green jersey – a little darker than the green of my dress – which perfectly suited his eyes. I wondered if it was an accident, or if he was perhaps a little vain or if his mother had chosen the jersey for him with care.

Joan and he and I were nervously sipping sherry when flamboyant Leo arrived. Seeing Timothy away from the familiar surroundings of school certainly made me a little awkward at first.

Joan opened the door to Leo whom she already knew and he came bursting into the sitting-room with cries of "My favourite un-married auntie!" and threw his arms around my neck and gave me an enormous kiss on both cheeks. So vehement was his greeting that he nearly threw me off my balance.

Leo looked his usual splendid self. His mane of fair hair was, I noticed, carefully and, no doubt, expensively, coloured with streaks of silver and mauve. I wondered what on earth Victor would have to say about that when he saw his son at Christmas.

I need not have worried about the conversation flagging for, just as I had hoped, Leo kept us entertained all evening with excited chatter about his drama school.

Timothy was rather quiet at first but a combination of Leo and a little wine soon helped him to relax. He became slightly flushed in the face and laughed loudly at Leo's stories. In fact I had never seen him so uninhibited.

The only problem with the whole evening was that we seemed to have prepared far too much food so that Joan and I were both horrified at the thought of all the left-overs.

Timothy didn't eat as much as I had expected and Leo announced as we sat down to supper that he was on a diet.

"I can't imagine why," I said. "You have a lovely slim figure."

"It's all on account of the aardvark," he said gesticulating wildly.

None of us knew exactly what an aardvark was although Timothy had a theory that it might be some sort of a pig. In fact he was not far wrong. It is, according to my dictionary, a termite-eating, nocturnal African mammal. We were at a loss to understand what this termite-eating mammal could possibly have to do with Leo.

It was merely, he explained, that he had to perform the part of an aardvark in class at college the following week. He had spent all week-end at London Zoo, studying the creature's habits.

I was a little disappointed as I had fondly imagined my nephew cast in the role of Hamlet – or if not Hamlet, at least Hotspur.

Timothy was delighted and revealed to my amazement that he too had occasional aspirations to go on the stage.

He ought, I suggested, to join the drama group at school, but he turned away and rather pointedly changed the subject.

The boys went away together quite soon after supper and although I was sorry to see them go so early I was happy to note that Leo seemed to be taking Timothy under his wing and hoped that perhaps they would see more of each other over the holidays.

As the boys left, I slipped a little packet into Timothy's hand.

"Just a little something for Christmas," I whispered in his ear.

He blushed and I felt ashamed at having caused him this embarrassment.

"It's only very little, nothing really," I said, making matters worse.

"Well, thanks a lot," he said, stuffing the packet into his pocket. "And thanks for the supper. It was great."

I closed the door behind them with a pang. All that work, I thought, all that laughing in the kitchen, all those nerves, all that food left over and the evening gone in the batting of an eyelid. I felt let down and a wave of sadness engulfed me. I wouldn't see Timothy again for over three weeks. Perhaps he would write to me to thank me for the little diary I had given him. He probably wouldn't. Children aren't very good at writing letters unless they are reminded.

It was silly of me to have given him that diary. What a dull present for a boy – and I had wrapped it up so carefully in such pretty Christmas paper.

It was not until I arrived to stay with Victor and Patricia on Christmas Eve that I heard from Leo about the final outcome of that evening.

Timothy, according to Leo, was a nice kid and Leo had taken him back to the flat which he shared with several other students, and there they had had more to drink. Suddenly it was rather late and when Timothy realised that he had missed the last tube he decided to stay the night. No one had enough money for a taxi.

The next morning they all slept until lunchtime so that when Timothy finally reached home his mother was in a terrible state. She had no idea where he was.

Timothy saw Leo again a few days later and told him all about

45

it. He hadn't supposed that his mother would notice his absence, or care if she did. She was usually out herself with one of her young men. Apparently she had a liking for boys. Timothy thought it disgusting.

I felt a curious twinge of jealousy at the thought of Timothy confiding in Leo as he never had in me. Then, I thought, children often don't confide in their parents. In any case I was delighted to think that the boys had made friends which, after all, had been my intention in the first place, and that I would to some extent be able to keep an eye on Timothy through Leo.

We talked a good deal about Timothy over Christmas, Leo and I. Leo liked him very much and I thought what a kind young man he was to bother about someone so much younger than himself.

*   *   *

Yesterday was the day when Eric and I were supposed to be going to Wells, but it was pouring with rain.

He rang me in the morning to say that it hardly seemed worth while setting out in such weather. We could always go another day.

"After all," he said, "we've got our whole lives in front of us," and laughed.

I agreed that the outing should be postponed and was pleasantly surprised to hear Eric say:

"Let's have a different outing today. Cheer ourselves up in this filthy weather. Would you like to come out to lunch? We might even go to the cinema afterwards. There's quite a good film on I'm told."

I was really quite touched.

So instead of going to Wells Cathedral we had a delicious Chinese meal in our local town, and spent the afternoon in the cinema watching what I suppose was quite a good film although I find it extremely difficult to cope with the ever-increasing amount of sexual activity to be seen in films these days. I was acutely embarrassed sitting there next to Eric, watching naked bodies writhing about on a celluloid bed.

Eric, on the other hand, didn't seem to mind at all.

CHAPTER
5

In a funny sort of way I find that lately I have begun to be quite disappointed if Eric doesn't come to see me fairly regularly. I can't think why, really, as he is not particularly stimulating company, and as I often find him remarkably irritating. Besides, as I never cease to remark, he frequently has his fly-buttons undone which to my mind is a sign of rapidly approaching senility. As often as not he tells me the same story over and over again — perhaps a story of no account concerning his wife and her prowess at housekeeping — or he merely resorts to the weather as a topic of conversation. To be fair though, I have to say that he does sometimes surprise me with an unexpected piece of esoteric knowledge about this plant or that bird, or some unexpected book which he may have read. But even so, I ask myself why am I so glad to see him shambling up the garden path? I am not, as I have pointed out, lonely; I am well able to cope with my own company, and, anyway, he invariably comes just when I am fully engrossed in some time-consuming operation such as writing or gardening.

I must admit that I am always grateful to him for his willingness to mend things for me — from the electric iron to the lavatory cistern — to carry in my coal and even to do the heavier jobs about the garden. Perhaps I also value the feeling of being needed and I suppose I feel that as a lonely widower, used to the permanent companionship of a woman, he does in some way need my company. He certainly seems to appreciate the little meal which I cook for him in return for all his kindness to me, not to mention the ginger cake I made for him last week.

And we do have some nice times together, bowling around the countryside in his old Ford Cortina and visiting little churches in hidden villages all over the county. Somerset is richly varied and although I have been connected with it for most of my life, there are still many lovely churches and glorious stretches of countryside as yet unknown to me. It is indeed a great pleasure, in later life, to have a companion with whom to explore these beauties.

On Monday afternoon we visited Isle Abbots where there is a gem of a church, quite outstanding in its simplicity and lightness. We were both moved by the peaceful beauty of this little church which stands among old cottages in an unspoilt village and so returned quietly contented to an early supper at my house.

Eric is clearly enjoying our forays into the countryside just as much as I am. At supper we pored over maps and books of local history in an attempt to decide where our next outing should take us.

It had been a nice day but as the evening drew in it became cold. There was surely a frost, I remarked, as we took our coffee over to the fireside. We had been sitting at the table for far too long.

One of the most irritating things about Eric is the way in which he eats. I have never ever known a man eat so slowly, with the result that I, who eat quite quickly, find myself sitting for hours over a meal with Eric, impatiently waiting for him to finish.

Like most people who eat slowly, he seems to devote a remarkable amount of concentration to the process. I have watched him dividing his food into neat little piles on his plate, frowning frantically lest each pile is not just as it should be, and carefully moving a Brussels sprout from one part of his plate to another. He will put one sprout, some potato and a piece of meat on his fork and lift the fork half way to his mouth before deciding that the balance of this particular mouthful is not exactly right, at which point he will slowly put down the fork, take the food off it and start again with a slightly smaller sprout or perhaps a little more potato. Once the food is finally in his mouth he chews it at least as many times as Gladstone would have done, making meanwhile a most unpleasant noise which is more reminiscent of a washing machine than anything else. When I think of what happens to my carefully prepared food when it is in Eric's mouth, I feel quite ill. Sometimes I wonder how I can bear ever to share a meal with the man.

So I was glad when we could at last leave the table.

As Eric sat down comfortably in the large armchair by the fire, I decided that the time had come for me to find out a little more about him. Something which I have been meaning to do for a while now.

"Eric," I said, "I think I have some brandy. How about a drop to keep out the cold?"

It is strangely difficult to get Eric to talk about himself. Perhaps he has some dark secret which he is frightened to divulge. But on the whole I think it would be nearer the truth to say that he is a naturally diffident man and one who perhaps thinks it ill-mannered to speak too much about himself. All that I really discovered from our fireside chat that evening was that he had spent a large part of his life working for Metal Boxes and, in so far as I could make out, living in various parts of the country. He had spent some years in Nottingham, others in Worksop and Ipswich. As a child he was brought up in Hertfordshire. I do not know at what age he married, nor what he did during the war and I was, of course, far too bashful to ask him where he went to school. But then there will be many more opportunities for questions of that nature.

Not only is Eric a diffident man who finds it perhaps distasteful to talk about himself, but he is extraordinarily incurious about others, or if not incurious, at least too well mannered to enquire.

He knows, of course, that I am a retired teacher, and he knows that my brother and sister-in-law, Victor and Patricia, live nearby. He knows, too, I think, that I was brought up in Somerset. But he knows these things only because I have volunteered them. I doubt that he has ever asked me a question which even vaguely touched upon the personal, and yet, for all that, I feel that he has a strong liking for me and a warm sympathy. He has a gentleness of manner which is not entirely unpleasing and which seems to betoken such a liking. He also has a peculiarly direct way of looking at me so that I hold his gaze with an unusual intimacy which leads me to suppose that he may feel that our friendship perhaps goes just beyond the bounds of humdrum, everyday casual companionship.

As far as I am concerned this is not true. I see the friendship precisely as a humdrum, casual companionship and I hope that Eric realises this, as the last thing I would wish to do would be to encourage him or to offend him.

When Eric left on Monday evening after drinking two glasses of my brandy, he stood at the front door and so, so gently, almost imperceptibly, squeezed my hand.

"You are very kind to me, Prudence," he said. "Thank you so much."

I was moved in a way and remained there in the lighted doorway, watching his unsteady figure lurching down the path to the garden gate.

*   *   *

After Christmas I returned to my house with a strange feeling of anti-climax. Two or three days with Victor and Patricia are enough so that I am usually glad to go home, to be my own master and to be among my own things. But on this occasion I felt somewhat loath to leave them. I decided that it was because of Leo. I was, and still am, very fond of Leo and he and I spent a good deal of time together over that Christmas.

Patricia was amazed that we had so much to say to each other.

Leo, she complained, rarely had a moment to spare to talk to his mother.

"What on earth do you two talk about?" she asked me. "And I do wish you would persuade him to stop doing such dreadful things to his hair. Victor is very upset about that."

51

Patricia lived in constant fear for her children. Perhaps all mothers do, but Patricia wore her fear on her sleeve.

"If Leo goes around looking like that," she said, "he will be mistaken for a criminal and be arrested — and you know the reputation the police have these days? They'll probably beat him up.'

I did my best to explain to Patricia that this was unlikely and that young people in the eighties no longer looked like they did when I, or indeed she, was young. But she appeared not to be listening.

Funnily enough it was not until that very moment that it occurred to me, with heart-stopping certainty, that Leo might have homosexual leanings so that his clearly very keen interest in Timothy surely had a side to it which had hitherto entirely escaped my notice.

For an instant I was horrified.

What had I done? Had I introduced an innocent child to a far from innocent young man who was about to seduce him — corrupt him — alter the course of his life for ever?

I felt a surge of panic. I was a school-teacher, a supposedly responsible member of society, entrusted with the care of young people; I should respect that trust, not play around with tender lives. But then as the panic ebbed away I realised that I was being quite ridiculous. Whatever Leo's tastes, he was unquestionably a nice young man and would certainly never dream of corrupting Timothy of whom he was obviously genuinely fond.

When I reached home I searched eagerly through the post which lay scattered on the floor in the hall. There were a couple of bills and a few late Christmas cards. Nothing else. Timothy had obviously not considered it worth his while to thank me for the diary. I could hardly blame him. It was a depressing little present, the thought of which embarrassed me. And yet, as day succeeded day, I found myself anxiously awaiting the postman just in case there was something from Timothy. I was so concerned to know if he had seen Leo again and, if so, how they were getting on. Besides I was worried about the boy lest he was unhappy, what with the troubles he had at home.

Finally, to my surprise, a letter did come on the last day of the holidays. Timothy was such a dear boy. So well mannered and thoughtful. He need not have written for I would not have minded at all and was indeed quite touched to think that he had bothered.

He thanked me for the supper at Joan's, for the dreary little diary and told me that the Christmas holidays hadn't been too bad in the end. That was all. No mention of Leo.

I could hardly, I thought, write to Leo enquiring about Timothy. It might seem a little peculiar, particularly as I would be seeing Timothy as soon as term started. In any case Leo would probably never get round to answering my letter. Neither did it occur to me to telephone Leo. I think I would have been rather tongue-tied ringing him merely to ask after Timothy.

The next day, in the late afternoon, the boarders began to reassemble for the Spring Term. I was not sure whether Timothy would be coming on the school train from Paddington which would be met by a coach at 4.30, or if he would be coming down by car with his mother − or perhaps even with his father. I had the impression that he usually came back to school on the train.

At half past four I chanced to find myself sorting tapes in the language laboratory whose windows looked out over the car park where the coach from the station would be arriving.

Every so often, out of idle curiosity, I would stroll over to the window and glance out, just to see what was going on.

I was standing, with a pile of tapes in my hands gazing out across the yard at the red brick monstrosity beyond, which was the main school building, and wondering if it was going to snow, when all of a sudden, and with a panache not usually associated with Blenkinsop's, a brand new Porsche, as I later discovered it to be, swept up the drive and came to a sudden halt just below the window where I stood.

My spectacles were a little misty so I put down the tapes, took off my glasses and polished them on my skirt. I was quite amazed when I put them back on my nose to recognise the young man who stepped out of the driver's seat as my nephew, Leo.

"Good Lord!" I thought on realising it was he. "What can be going on?"

Next the front passenger seat door opened and an extraordinarily elegant leg appeared, followed by another and Timothy's mother, clad in furs, emerged from the car.

"Where do we go now, darling?" I heard her piping tones.

Timothy himself was just clambering out of the back of the car, struggling with a duffle bag and a hockey stick.

"Well I never!" I thought to myself, and, with a sense of pique: "They might have told me!"

Leo glanced around him and, as he did so, I stepped back from the window not wishing to be seen by any one of them.

I watched as the three of them walked away across the yard towards the red brick monstrosity. Then I went and sat down at a desk. I took off my spectacles and leaned back in the chair, wondering what to do next. I decided that Leo would obviously want to see me and would be bound to call at my house, so I had better go home. I could not think why he had not warned me of his coming since he might easily have missed me altogether.

As soon as I reached my house I closed the curtains, stoked up the fire and tried to make the sitting-room as welcoming as possible. Outside it was bitterly cold.

I looked at my watch. It was half past five. I decided to make a pot of tea while I waited. Perhaps Leo would arrive in time to share it with me. I wondered if he would bring Timothy's mother and Timothy with him. He might well. I did not like the thought of Timothy's mother, but I have to admit that I was extremely curious to meet her.

By half past six no one had appeared. I thought that perhaps they had called earlier on their way to school, but imagined that, even if they had, they would be bound to come back again. I was beginning to feel restless. I had finished my tea a long time ago and didn't know what to do next. I fed Pansy. I tried distractedly to read the newspaper but found that I was hardly concentrating on anything I read, so I eventually turned on the television. Nothing there seemed to hold my interest.

Suddenly the telephone rang. Ah . . . I sprang to my feet. That must be they, I thought, ringing to find out if I am in.

It was one of the assistant French teachers wanting to know how the third year was coping with the syllabus.

At half past seven I decided that it was too early for supper. I began to open all the cupboards in the kitchen to see if I had any food to offer Leo — Timothy — Timothy's mother — whoever might turn up. There wasn't very much.

By half past eight I was beginning to feel a little angry. I should not have spent the whole evening at home. I had not finished the job I had been doing in the language laboratory and besides, under normal circumstances, I would have been in the common room. Not only pupils, but other members of staff often used to look for one on the first evening of term. I could still go back to school, but then I hadn't yet eaten and I really didn't want to miss Leo, if he turned up. He must surely turn up, but I did wonder what on earth he had been doing since arriving at school several hours ago.

Patricia, it occurred to me, would have had a fit if she had seen the way Leo drove that Porsche.

No one came to see me that night. The telephone rang once more. It was the headmaster with some trivial, self-important request; and the television went on the blink. I went to bed crossly a little after eleven and tossed and turned until I finally fell asleep in the small hours.

I was hardly in the best of moods the following morning. More than anything else, I felt hurt. It seemed quite inconceivable to me that Leo should have come to the school without having made himself known to me. The fact that he had come with Timothy and Timothy's mother only added insult to injury since, after all, it was I who had introduced him to Timothy.

The best interpretation which I could put on the whole affair was that they had called on me early in the afternoon, and found me out. I still felt that they should have tried again later.

Leo, I felt, was very much to blame, but in my heart I longed to let him off the hook, so I partly excused him on grounds of his youth and also because he probably felt that, since he was driving her car, he was in Timothy's mother's hands.

As for Timothy's mother, I had no time for her. She must have known how concerned I had been over her son and that I had indeed taken him under my wing. It seemed to me that the least she could have done would have been to make herself known to me.

As I went into the common room I was feeling particularly irritable and the first person I saw was Timothy's housemaster who looked at me with what can only be described as an insolent stare and said,

"Your little toy boy's back, Prudence — I met his mother yesterday. Quite a corker."

The tastelessness of the man was unbearable. In fact it was the first time that I had heard the expression 'toy boy' and have to admit that I had, then, no idea of the connotations of the phrase.

I said good-morning to one or two other colleagues before the headmaster came in dressed in a gown, ready for assembly.

He cleared his voice and spoke to the room in general.

"It has come to my notice," he said, "that there is too much sexual activity going on in the school — particularly among the fourth formers." He paused. "This must not," he added, "be discussed outside these walls as I should not like prospective — or indeed present — parents to become aware of the problem. I shall be taking serious steps to curb this unfortunate trend, and so with this in mind I propose to announce at Assembly that from now onwards the six inch rule will be extended to ten and a half inches."

There was a school rule which forbade pupils of the opposite sex from walking within six inches of one another.

"That's bound to do the trick, Headmaster," I said drily.

The Headmaster stared at me balefully over his half-moon spectacles and said,

"How else would you deal with the problem, Prudence?"

I was not really interested in sexual intercourse in the fourth form at that moment for I was far more concerned about

Timothy whom I would be teaching later that morning, and his mother and Leo.

"I sometimes just think good luck to them," I said with a weary sigh. And the bell rang for Assembly.

*   *   *

Patricia is in a terrible state. Her daughter, Laurel, has shaved off all her hair as a sign that she disapproves of men and has no intention of attracting them.

If only Laurel knew how hard it is in life to attract the ones you want, she might not do anything so rash. Quite apart from that she is scarcely an appealing child and should not really have any problems in that direction. I hardly imagine that she is surrounded by a flock of unwanted admirers.

Be that as it may, Patricia was in floods of tears on the telephone. I did my best to console her. Laurel's hair would soon grow again, more luxuriantly than ever, I assured her.

"Why can't my children leave their heads alone?" Patricia wailed. She begged me to come over and talk to Laurel as she felt that I might have some influence where she had failed.

Since Laurel had already shaved her head I could hardly see what use there could be in my talking to her. But Patricia was determined that I should come. Even if I had no effect on Laurel, I might be of some consolation to Victor who, in disgust at his daughter's behaviour, now not only refused to eat his meals with her, but closed his eyes whenever he saw her.

Eventually, much against my wishes, I agreed to go and spend a long week-end with Victor and Patricia.

There was no doubt about it that Laurel looked perfectly dreadful with her head shaven like Yul Brynner's.

When I first saw her, she had just come in from school and I have to admit that if I had not known it was she, I would not instantly have recognised her.

I decided to make no comment.

Victor, who was sitting with me at the time, watching the six o'clock news on television, immediately rose from his chair, put his hands over his eyes, and without further comment stumbled out of the room, tripping over a footstool and bumping into the door jamb on his way. Throughout the four days in which I stayed with my bother, he continued to avoid his daughter in just this manner.

"What," he said to me in private, "have we done? Leo a few years ago had a shock of purple curls, and now Laurel is as bald as a coot." For a moment I thought he was going to cry.

Patricia did cry — at regular intervals throughout the week-end. Neither she nor Victor could see that all was not lost, that Laurel was surely just going through a phase, and nor did they think it in the least little bit funny when two of her girlfriends called to see her on Saturday, both of whom had taken the same drastic measure.

For me it was a dreary week-end. The outing I had been planning with Eric for the Saturday had to be cancelled, which did not really matter except that I felt I was letting him down, and I was certainly achieving nothing with Victor and Patricia.

When I eventually came home, free at last from Patricia's hysterical moaning and from Victor's idiotic despair, I telephoned Eric only to find that he was out. I rang again a few hours later and still there was no reply.

It is ridiculous that I should in any way depend on Eric — and far be it from me to suppose that I do — but there is something slightly annoying about a person being out whom one rather expects to be not only in, but urgently awaiting one's call.

Eric has been away for three days now and I do vaguely wonder where he can have gone.

CHAPTER
6

With Eric not here to interrupt me, I have all the time in the
world to get on with my writing.

*　　　*　　　*

It was with a remarkable feeling of inadequacy, as if I were
setting out on some unknown, perilous trail, ill-equipped for
what might lie ahead, that I approached the classroom where
Timothy and some twenty-five others were awaiting their first
French lesson that term. In some indefinable way the balance of
power between Timothy and myself had shifted, leaving me
insecure and uncertain how to behave next. No one, least of all a
member of the teaching profession, likes to find himself in this
position.

I could not, of course, discuss my nephew, nor the holidays,
nor anything else pertaining to life outside school, in the classroom. I had to behave as though nothing untoward had occurred
and try to teach the class with my habitual authority.

That class seemed to last for an eternity and I did not, I know,
teach it with anything like my habitual authority. I kept forgetting
what we were doing, I made elementary blunders and whenever
a child put a question to me, I had to ask him or her to repeat it
as I seemed to have the greatest difficulty in comprehending the
simplest enquiry. I avoided catching Timothy's eye and was at
the same time hurt by the certainty that he, too, was avoiding

catching mine. I longed for the class to come to an end, and yet I dreaded it lest I had not managed to speak to Timothy before the bell rang. If I were to speak, I wondered if I would dare to suggest that he come round for tea.

When the bell did eventually ring, the children all gathered up their books with the usual banging and clattering and, like an untidy bunch of unkempt puppies, they pushed and shoved their way out of the room.

I sat for a while at my desk, carefully replacing the lid of my fountain pen, neatly piling my books, folding my spectacles and putting them away in their case.

Timothy left the room with the others, without so much as a backward glance.

The next day I taught Timothy's class again. And the next. And by Saturday, which was the fourth day, I still had not managed to have a private word with him. I was angry not so much with him as with myself. It seemed quite ridiculous to me that a middle-aged school teacher should find herself in such a ludicrous position vis à vis a pupil of some fourteen or fifteen years.

I could no longer sleep at night and lay awake for hours wondering exactly why it was that Timothy had not been to see me and why it was that he had so obviously avoided me.

And what about Leo?

I went over and over and over the question of Leo until the whole episode had assumed gigantic proportions in my imagination. It seemed as if, all at once, everyone was turning against me. Even my own kith and kin. I almost felt as though I had no friends. Certainly those in whom I had always trusted would probably think me most peculiar were I to confide in them my worries concerning Timothy. After all, what exactly were those worries? What precisely was the problem?

So I spent the first week-end of term closeted in my house with Pansy. She sat on my knee and I entrusted my anxieties to her whilst she, as is the custom with Pekineses, alternately snored and allowed me to feed her with chocolate drops.

As I stroked Pansy's head and fed her yet another chocolate

drop, the thought occurred to me that I was being completely idiotic. Here I was, a middle-aged professional woman living alone with a Pekinese in whom I had lately, although never before, taken to confiding.

And of what stuff were these confidences? Anyone reading my mind might have supposed that I was in love with Timothy. I blushed as I dared so much as to formulate the thought to myself. In my embarrassment I stood up and paced nervously around the room.

The very idea was, of course, utterly absurd. It is quite inconceivable that a woman in her mid-fifties, as I was then, should fall in love with a mere child. The fact that I had even allowed the denial of such a supposition to flit through my mind was deeply upsetting and acutely uncomfortable.

There are times in one's life when one is more than usually glad that no one, not even one's dog, can read one's thoughts. This was just such a moment.

Of course I have, in, my lifetime, fallen in love other than with the fictional characters I have mentioned. When I was only about thirteen or fourteen I developed a tremendous passion for a handsome older cousin who must have regarded me as a mere child and who was later killed in the war. Then at university I fell very much in love with one of our lecturers, and there have naturally been other moments when my heart has missed a beat, but, as I have already explained, love, or at least the expression of it, is something which, on the whole, has passed me by.

I know perfectly well that I was not 'in love' with Timothy. How could I have been?

And yet from this time onwards I was beleaguered by people who supposed that I was. Or, if they did not suppose it, they thought it amusing to pretend that they did and to make distasteful jokes at my expense on the subject.

By the end of my solitary week-end with only Pansy for company, and in fact before I had been greeted by the full horror of public opinion, I had decided that I must pull myself together, as it were, stop being so negative, and invite Timothy to tea. When he came, as he surely would, I could casually ask him about Leo, and even mention the fact that I had seen Leo from the language laboratory window on that first evening of term.

On Monday morning I happened to come across Timothy in the corridor. I stopped to talk to him and, as I did so, was infuriated to hear a vulgar wolf whistle coming from a passing lout. 'Lout' is the only word I can think of suitably to describe such a boy. The lout's companion, another uncouth creature, sniggered and the two of them walked on.

I, of course, pretended to have noticed nothing.

Timothy, whom I had somehow expected to be embarrassed when confronted by me, smiled a disarming smile and promised to come and see me that very afternoon.

When he arrived I was not altogether surprised to find him more than usually despondent. He sat limply on the sofa.

The holidays, he said, hadn't been bad. Leo had been jolly kind to him, but, and he looked down at his long legs stretched out in front of him and shuffled his feet awkwardly, he hated being back at school.

I could never really get to the bottom of why Timothy was so unhappy at school. He should, in my opinion, have overcome his initial shyness and begun to make friends.

He claimed that he could never fit in. Somehow − and he seemed to have an amazingly mature understanding of the situation − he had got off to a bad start. People had begun by being vile to him, perhaps because he had arrived late his first term, or perhaps just because they didn't like his face. It had become a habit.

He had thought at first that if he tried at games he would be better liked, but the only result of his efforts in that direction was that he seemed to become even more unpopular. A group of two or three bullies had systematically rifled his locker in the changing room and pee-ed on his Rugby shorts and even into his Rugby boots.

I was appalled. Why hadn't he reported the incident?

Such incidents, he said, staring at me gravely from under a lock of red-gold hair, always go unreported. The only thing to do is to keep quiet, mind your own business and hope to pass unnoticed. He consoled himself by writing poetry. He had always done that and now he was writing a short story. One day perhaps he would be a professional writer.

He looked at me again and said,

"You know, they even tease me for coming to see you."

"That is ridiculous," I said sharply, and shifted uncomfortably in my chair.

"It's just that here it's like a proper house," he said by way of explanation. "Not like school. It doesn't smell of disinfectant and school food."

Well, that was at least something, I thought.

I decided to take the plunge.

"Did Leo bring you back to school on Tuesday evening?" I asked suddenly.

"No," said Timothy frankly, looking straight at me. "Why should he have?"

"I have no idea why he should have," I said, "But I merely thought that I caught sight of him in the car park."

Timothy looked at his hands and picked at what was probably a wart.

"If he'd been here," he said, still staring at his hands, "surely he'd have come to see you."

"I would have thought so," I said tartly, and added, "What did you do with him in the holidays?"

"Nothing much. We just used to hang around at his place quite a lot and watch videos. We went to a pop concert once."

"Did you invite him to meet your mother?" I asked.

Timothy looked straight at me again, almost suspiciously, I thought.

"Yes," he said, "he met my mother."

There was an awkward silence and then Timothy added,

"I hate my mother."

As he spoke he blushed and, for a moment, looked near to tears.

"How can you hate your mother?" I wanted to know, and added feebly, "I'm sure she's very fond of *you*."

I had no idea whether Timothy's mother had any fondness for

her son or not, but I had certainly never pictured her, since that first day in the Secretary's office, as epitomising mother love. All the same this was the first time in my life that I had heard a child articulate such a terrible emotion. When I was at school no girl would have dreamed of expressing herself in such terms. And, of course, these are not the usual terms in which a pupil speaks to a teacher.

"I've got to go," said Timothy, standing up suddenly. "But can I come again at the week-end?"

"Tea on Sunday," I said firmly, glad to be back on safe ground.

"Thanks a lot," he said, making for the door.

"Bring a friend, if you want," I offered.

He turned round and looked at me fiercely.

"I don't have any friends. Not here anyway," he said, "and I hate my mother. She's a cow."

I really felt rather relieved as I shut the door behind Timothy. What on earth, I wondered, had got into the boy that he should feel so much anger and resentment. He had always before given me the impression of a pained child who laboured certainly under some resentments, but nothing so extreme as this.

How could I help him, I wondered. And why the lies about Leo whom it almost seemed as if he was protecting?

It crossed my mind that there might be something between Leo and Mrs Hooper, but the idea seemed preposterous. She was a young and very pretty woman who could surely do better than to pick up an eighteen-year-old boy with purple hair, although there was no doubt about it that Leo was an extremely good-looking eighteen-year-old. But good-looking or not, he seemed like a baby to me; not at all grown-up. But then I had known him all my life and perhaps he managed to disguise his lack of sophistication when meeting outsiders. Whichever way I looked at it, though, it seemed absurd to suppose that there could be any kind of friendship between two such unlikely people.

I put the idea out of my mind but, in doing so, I have to admit that I allowed myself once again to dwell on the possibility of a homosexual link between Leo and Timothy.

64

Something, I felt sure, was afoot and if it wasn't Timothy's mother and Leo it must be Leo and Timothy. Of the two possibilities, I am sorry to say that I inclined towards the second as being the likelier.

Then I spent a long time wondering which of the two liaisons I personally found more disturbing.

I have to admit that the idea of Siren Hooper seducing my innocent young nephew entirely filled me with horror, whereas I could well understand that Leo might have developed a, surely platonic, passion for young Timothy. The idea was disturbing but not totally distasteful as I could easily understand Leo's feeling. Timothy was such an innocent, clean boy, quite pure, unspoiled in his thinking, and physically pleasing. Neither could I help remembering, with a faint feeling of unease, the incident of Timothy's homosexual sonnet.

The frail, young child I had once seen in the Secretary's office, had turned into a nice-looking, sensitive youth. His green eyes and his red-gold hair lent him an almost angelic look, although I have to admit that lately his child's body seemed to have become more essentially male.

I must not, I thought, as I took out my pen to begin marking a pile of sixth form essays on Camus's L'Etranger, allow myself to become unduly preoccupied with the boy. And yet, as with half a mind I marked those papers, the haunting vision of Timothy kept reappearing in my imagination.

I saw him blushing, nearly crying as he announced his hatred of his mother.

I saw him as he was at the very beginning . . . small and frail.

I saw him eating crumpets, chocolate cake . . . roly poly pudding . . . pitta bread. I saw him cramming that silly diary into his pocket, thanking me for tea, smiling at me, looking at me from under his red-gold fringe, I saw him stretching his lanky legs out in front of him, taking a bisuit with his long, thin, pale hands, picking his wart, handing in his prep, clambering out of the back seat of a Porsche, singing in the choir . . . I could not get him out of my mind – and I cannot imagine why, for there was nothing really extraordinary about Timothy – except perhaps for his eyes, his eyes were very green. But then his eyes were hardly any concern of mine.

"Meursault," I read in a neat, round, childish, girl's hand, as I tried again to concentrate on the sixth form essays in front of me, "was condemned to death, not so much for the murder of the Arabs on the beach, as for not having cried at his mother's funeral . . .'

I wondered if Timothy would cry at his mother's funeral. *Aujourd'hui, maman est morte. Ou peut être hier* . . . Suddenly I realised that Timothy reminded me very much of Meursault. He was like Meursault in almost every way. Timothy was an Outsider, a kind of free soul . . .

It must have been at about this point that I put down my pen and buried my head in my hands.

Perhaps it was living alone which finally warped the intelligence.

What on earth was I doing comparing my pupil to characters in fiction? Would I soon be seeing myself as Phaedra, guiltily in love with young, forbidden fruit?

"*C'est Venus toute entière à sa proie attachée* . . ."

"Oh God," I thought, pushing the papers angrily away from me and getting up from the table. I must really be going mad. "It must be the winter," I thought . . . my age . . . the silence . . . the tedium of the children's essays.

Why did I keep thinking of love in that silly way? I was not interested in love except as a subject for literature.

Clearly I had a touch of 'flu'. It was hardly surprising at that time of year and with the weather as cold as it was. I would make myself a hot drink and go to bed. I would surely be more myself in the morning.

Sunday eventually came, and early in the afternoon, just as I was preparing tea, the door bell rang. I looked at my watch. I had not expected Timothy for at least half an hour and even then he would probably be late as he was generally on the unpunctual side.

I took off my apron, glanced at myself in the hall mirror and patted my hair as I passed. Not looking any younger, I thought grimly, and hurried on to open the door, with Pansy yapping at my heels.

To my surprise, when I opened it, there, on the front step, stood Leo. He wore an enormous moth-eaten astrakhan coat which he could only have acquired at some flea-market — or perhaps Oxfam — and a Russian hat from beneath which escaped a few stray lilac and magenta curls. On his feet he had a pair of bright pink Wellington boots.

"Good gracious me!" I said. "What a surprise! Come on in."

Leo came in, took off his coat to reveal a blue boiler suit and gave me a big kiss.

"What *would* your father say?" I asked, gazing in amazement at him. "You look quite extraordinary!"

"He'd probably burst into tears," said Leo nonchalantly, and added, "What's for tea, Auntie?"

"Well," I replied somewhat hesitantly, "I was rather expecting Timothy — but it's a bit on the early side for him yet."

"The bad news," said Leo, sitting down at my kitchen table and staring greedily at a fruit cake I'd made the evening before, "is that Timothy's not coming. You've got me instead."

I felt, for an instant, a slight feeling of panic.

Why wasn't Timothy coming? What had happened? Why hadn't he let me know? Perhaps I had offended him in some way . . .

Then I managed to bring my attention back to Leo, sitting there looking at the cake, dressed in a boiler suit with his pink hair and pink boots and Russian hat.

"Go on," I said, "cut yourself a slice. I'll make the tea."

As I put the tea-leaves in the pot, I asked him what exactly had brought him to Blenkinsop's. Not just affection for his old aunt, I couldn't help thinking.

"Marietta Hooper's Porsche," he said.

Marietta! What a ridiculous name, I thought.

I said, "Not again!" I don't know why I said it, for I hate to catch people lying, and I dared not turn round to look at him.

Leo did what was possibly the best possible thing to do under the circumstances, which was to affect not to hear.

"She lets me drive it," he said. "Incredible car! Amazing acceleration!" He told me in how many fractions of a second it could go from 0 to 100 m.p.h. I was not interested.

"Why is she so keen to allow you to drive her car?" I asked, turning round at last and putting the teapot on the table.

"Lust," said Leo with a ludicrous wiggle of his shoulders.

"What on earth are you talking about?" I wanted to know, although in fact I knew, of course. It was just as I had imagined. Oh dear! I felt rather sick.

My hand began to tremble slightly as I poured the tea. I wasn't sure what to say. I am, I flatter myself, more worldly wise and a great deal less easily shockable than my brother, Victor, but I still felt that somehow I ought to be dissuading my young nephew from embarking on a career as a gigolo.

"I mean," said Leo, "that she fancies me something rotten."

"How can you be so sure?" I asked. "Perhaps she just lets you drive her car out of kindness."

"Perhaps," said Leo, "she leans her heavily scented body against mine and runs her hand up my thigh and her fingers through my amazingly beautiful curls out of kindness, too."

"Leo!" I said. "You are awful! I'm sure she doesn't." I was dreadfully embarrassed.

Leo leaned across the table and gave me a genuinely sweet smile.

"Don't worry, Auntie," he said, "there's no danger. She won't seduce me because, you see, women aren't my scene." He made a mocking, self-deprecatory camp gesture.

Then he suddenly looked serious and said kindly,

"I'm sorry, I haven't shocked you, have I?"

"Not in the least bit," I said. "I had half suspected it in any case. But it would shock me very much indeed if I thought you were leading Mrs Hooper on just for what you could get out of her. That would not be very nice." I paused and gave him what I hoped was a penetrating look, and said, "What exactly are you planning to get out of her?"

"Nothing," he said, "nothing."

I gave him another long, hard stare.

It was time, I realised, that I came to the point.

"Leo," I said, "I saw you getting out of that car on the first night of term with Timothy and his mother. I don't mind the fact that you didn't come to see me but I do mind the fact that both you and Timothy lied to me. People only lie when they have something to hide."

Leo was back in his usual ebullient form in no time. Of course they had nothing to hide. They were in a tremendous hurry, didn't want to hurt me, had to pick up a puppy in Basingstoke, drop a case of champagne in Hampstead, collect a dress from the cleaners, make a transatlantic telephone call, go out to dinner, catch a train and a thousand other unlikely things. Of course they had had a puncture on the way down and on top of all that, poor Marietta had been suffering from an appalling head-ache all day long.

Mrs Hooper had come to take Timothy out today, and so Leo had taken the opportunity to come with her to see me and to make things up with me. Timothy and his mother were having tea in the town.

I didn't suppose for one minute that Leo had come for that reason alone and I told him so.

"Of course," he admitted, "I'm always quite pleased to see Timothy. He's a good kid." And then he went back to describing the joys of driving that horrible car.

Neither, when I came to think about it, did I suppose that Mrs Hooper had come just to take out her son. She had never, in so far as I could remember, shown any interest in taking him out from school before.

No. There was something not very nice going on. The mother wanted Leo and Leo wanted the son.

Truth, I thought to myself, is indeed stranger than fiction.

When Leo finally left, I said, as I kissed him goodbye,

"Please behave yourself Leo, and don't do anything silly."

"Me do something silly? Never!" he said. "Watch this," and he dived into the driving seat of the beastly Porsche which turned out to be parked right outside my front door, and with a spurt of low-slung power and a merry wave from the window, disappeared down the narrow street.

It was very cold outside. I shivered as I closed the front-door and drew the bolt.

The whole lot of them, I thought, worry me. They worry me to death. And when, just when would I next have a chance to see Timothy alone . . .?

CHAPTER
7

Patricia has an annoying habit of always telephoning with her latest dramas and worries just as I am on the point of going out.

Eric was away again for two or three days last week and by the time he came back I have to admit that I was beginning to miss his familiar, shambling figure coming up the path, although I did manage to get a certain amount of writing done while he was away. To tell the truth, I badly needed him, in my selfish way, to replace a cracked pane of glass in the bathroom window.

Eric is a very kind man and he came round to do that almost immediately. I was so grateful to him that I begged him to stay for lunch. I do not like to think of Eric being so often alone in his own house.

Lately I have been getting to know Eric rather better. We have been on several trips together and it seems to me that when he is away from home he relaxes and becomes more expansive. I am beginning to know a little more about him and to see a new and likeable side to him. A side which is strangely light-hearted for a man of his age – almost to the point of childishness.

I have discovered that Eric likes music and so one evening we drove down to Exeter together to hear a concert of Baroque music in the cathedral there, and we have plans to go to other concerts together in future.

When Eric came to replace my window pane he mentioned that while he was away he had gone with a friend to a wonderful performance of *The Magic Flute*. She was a great opera lover.

She . . .?

I wondered, with something closely resembling a pang of jealousy, who 'she' was.

But I must not be ridiculous. I have no claim to Eric's sole attention and, indeed, if I did have it, I would find it sorely irritating.

Our next plan was to go for a day to the South Coast. Neither of us had ever been to Lyme Regis. So on Tuesday morning (the day before yesterday) I was just putting on my coat and was about to leave the house when the telephone rang.

Needless to say it was Patricia and needless to say she was in tears again.

"Patricia, my dear," I said as kindly as I could, "you are lucky to have caught me. I am just about to go out."

Patricia paid no attention at all. As far as she was concerned I might not have spoken.

"Prudence," she said between gulped back tears, "you must come . . . it's Laurel again . . . I really don't know what to do with her . . . Victor is out of his mind with worry. He thinks we should call in a psychiatrist. What would you do? You must know about these things."

It always seems to Patricia that because of my experiences as a school teacher I have the ultimate answer to all adolescent problems. Anyway I realised that I was not going to get away in a hurry as she was deeply distressed and clearly had to talk to someone.

Laurel, it appears, is so angry with her father for steadfastly refusing to look at her for several weeks now, ever since she began shaving her head, that she has decided to make a protest. The protest involves walking around the house entirely naked whenever she is alone with her parents.

As far as I could see this can only be of inconvenience to Laurel herself, since she must feel not only cold, but utterly silly as well.

Anyway I hadn't heard the worst part of the whole thing. The worst part of the whole thing is that in order to show her sympathy with the Greenpeace movement, Laurel has dyed her body hair green.

The picture is not a pretty one. Laurel is not a thin child and her head is at present as bald as an egg.

Patricia wept. There is nothing she can say which could possibly have any influence on the girl. Victor has taken to eating his meals in his bedroom for fear of encountering his daughter and whenever he does move about the house from one room to another, he does so with his eyes tight shut. As far as Patricia is concerned it is like living with two lunatics, although she admitted that the sight of Laurel alternately incenses and disgusts her to such an extent that she, too, has taken to closing her eyes when addressing her daughter.

For Patricia it is not so much the emerald green pubic hair as the pea-green under-arm hair that she finds really offensive. Had I any idea quite how many different shades of green there are . . .?

Patricia began to sound quite hysterical. She was sobbing as she talked, and she was talking quite incomprehensibly about spinach and sage and avocados and olive − yes olive − and beech and apple and lime and lettuce and moss and bottle . . . and even the sea got a mention. I thought she would go on for ever.

I was longing to put down the telephone and to go and meet Eric although I have to admit that this time even I was somewhat upset to hear of Laurel's excesses, and worried, too, by Patricia. She seemed to be hovering dangerously near the brink. She was apparently quite unable to stop crying.

The telephone is hardly the best medium for serious conversations of any kind, but when I finally managed to interrupt Patricia, I did my very best to console her.

There was no knowing to what ends teenagers were prepared to go to annoy their parents these days.

"But teenagers didn't exist when we were young," wailed Patricia.

"I know," I said, "of course they didn't. They were invented after the war and, like every other intolerable modern horror, brought over from America."

I told her that I absolutely could not go and see her immediately as I was going out to lunch and for the afternoon with Eric.

She asked me where we were going and then begged me to come to supper in the evening.

After a long day I felt that I would really be too tired to go out again in the evening, but Patricia was insistent. We could have an early supper, she said, and I could bring Eric. We could come on our way back from Lyme Regis.

I wondered what Eric would make of Victor and Patricia and wondered, too, if I really wanted to effect an introduction. There is something to be said, I sometimes think, for keeping one's life compartmentalised. It also occurred to me that Eric might not want me to accept on his behalf.

But Patricia went on and on and eventually it seemed to me that the only way of getting her off the telephone was to agree to what she wanted.

We would come early, I said, on our way home from Lyme Regis, unless I rang to the contrary which I would only do if Eric couldn't for some reason come.

Patricia was delighted. She still sounded rather over-excited, but at least she had stopped crying. She was so relieved, she said, because it would mean that for this evening, if only for this evening, Laurel would put some clothes on and Victor would be able to have supper downstairs, even if he insisted on keeping his eyes shut to avoid seeing his daughter's bald head.

At last Patricia rang off. I looked at my watch. Poor Eric had been kept waiting. We were going in my car for a change and I had promised to come and pick him up.

I had to explain to Eric why I had so rudely kept him waiting and so, as we bowled along in my little car and rather against my better judgment, I embarked on the whole story about Laurel. Perhaps I felt that I owed it to him if he was to be dragged over to Victor's and Patricia's for supper, although it is not usual for me to discuss my family with outsiders.

Half way through the story about Laurel's pubic hair I found myself floundering about for words. I was not at all sure what Eric would make of so indelicate a story and thought, too, that

74

he might well be shocked by my telling it. In fact Eric's reaction was one of tremendous mirth. I have never seen him laugh quite so heartily. When I told him that Patricia had insisted on our coming to supper, he was nothing short of overjoyed.

For a moment the old school-mistress in me came to the fore.

"Laurel will be properly dressed," I said, looking at him sharply, "when we get there."

"You have to give it to them," he said. "These young people — if you can't beat them, join them."

Eric is a man for whom a cliché is always a treasure. He produces them at every possible opportunity. They lard his conversation seemingly so as to protect him from the real world and its emotions: the devil you know . . .; life is what you make it; it wouldn't do for us all to be the same; if you can't beat them, join them, and so on for ever. I wondered if, on this occasion, he had bothered to consider what he was saying for even one fraction of a second.

"The last thing we want to do in this instance," I said tartly, "is to join them."

I began to regret having told Eric about the episode at all. He had what I interpreted as a faintly salacious look on his face, which I found both distasteful and annoying and for which I knew that I was partly responsible. I did hope that our day out was not about to be spoiled.

I decided to change the subject.

"Have you seen *The French Lieutenant's Woman*?" I asked brightly. "It was filmed in Lyme Regis, I believe."

The day had got off to a maddening start and I was feeling somewhat irritable and consequently annoyed with myself, but it was not long before Eric's good humour communicated itself to me. I don't know whether or not his cheerfulness was caused by my telling him about Laurel and by the knowledge that he was going to meet her in the evening. Perhaps he was just pleased to be going out.

It was a bright, windy day and we drove down to the coast through delightful countryside reaching Lyme by late morning, just in time to visit the fossil museum before having lunch in a pub. After lunch we enjoyed a walk along the Cob and then we set off home via Axmouth and Axminster. It was a long drive and Eric sat there beside me chattering and laughing and producing clichés all day long.

He talked about his son, which he had hardly ever done before. He spoke of how he had missed him a lot when he first went to Australia. But he was used to being without him now. You can't win them all, he said. And he talked about his own childhood in Hertfordshire, about his doctor father and his clever mother. His only brother, an identical twin of whom he was inordinately fond, was killed in a motor bicycle accident in early manhood. A shadow crossed the sun. He had been a young man full of promise with a talent for painting and a remarkable zest for life. It had been a terrible waste.

"Ah well," said Eric, "we'll all be dead in a hundred years."

"Much sooner than that," I replied, and Eric's spirits were instantly restored. The sun came out again.

We needed to stop for petrol and began to watch out for a garage on our side of the road. It was not very long before we came to a large, prosperous, modern-looking monstrosity with a shop attached.

As Eric filled the car with petrol I wandered into the shop, thinking that I might find a chamois leather. I had been meaning to buy one for the car for some time. I was searching blankly among a peculiar assortment of nylon knickers inscribed with vulgar slogans and cheap sherry glasses when Eric arrived to pay for the petrol.

We began to argue slightly about whose turn it was to pay when Eric suddenly said,

"How extraordinary! Listen to the tune they're playing. That takes me right back to my youth." And he began to sing, "When your heart's on fire, You must realise, Smoke gets in your eyes . . ." Before I knew what was happening I had allowed him to take me in his arms and there we went whirling around the shop floor.

I was dressed in my maroon, belted overcoat and was wearing flat, lace-up walking shoes on my rather large feet. Eric, who is a little shorter than I, was wearing his mack and some rather nasty brown plastic gloves with strange holes punched in the backs — presumably for purposes of aeration. He had a funny little narrow-brimmed tweed hat on his head and as we danced he peered at me intently over the rims of his spectacles.

We must have looked very peculiar to the woman at the till and to a young couple who were standing there hand in hand examining a display of cellophane-wrapped sandwiches.

It was all over in an instant and as we came to a halt by the till, I felt myself blushing to the roots of my hair. Without looking around, I disengaged myself from Eric and walked quickly out into the forecourt, leaving him to pay for the petrol. I had never done anything so extraordinary in all my life before.

When Eric got back into the car he laughed and then apologised. He hadn't intended to embarrass me. It didn't matter, I said. I was just rather surprised.

"You're only young once," he said. The more I see of Eric, the stranger I find him. He is not quite the dull, unimaginative man I initially took him for. But then, as he would say, you can't tell a book by its cover.

We drove on for a while in silence. It was as though Eric's euphoria had been spent in the dance. I caught sight of him out of the corner of my eye. He looked thoughtful. Perhaps he was thinking of his lost youth, lost wife, lost brother, lost child. I wondered. Perhaps he was just tired. Or perhaps he was thinking about his opera-going friend. I wondered about her too, but I dared not ask. What Eric did when he was away was none of my business.

I was certainly tired, and I was not particularly looking forward to an evening with Victor and Patricia. But at the very mention of Victor and Patricia, Eric came to life again.

He was really looking forward to meeting my brother and sister-in-law.

When we arrived, quite early, at my brother's house we found Patricia in the kitchen. Victor had not yet come in from work. He seemed to come home later and later these days. Patricia rather supposed that it was in order to avoid Laurel.

We went into the sitting-room and Patricia offered us a drink.

Eric gladly accepted a gin and tonic. I thought that I would wait and perhaps just have some wine with dinner.

Patricia said that she must go back to the kitchen and I offered to help her, supposing her to be anxious to speak to me in private.

Eric said that he would be quite happy with his drink and *The Times* which was lying on the coffee table in front of him.

In the kitchen Patricia mashed potatoes whilst I vaguely stirred the soup and listened to her litany of despair.

There was no knowing what Laurel would do next. Mind you she could hardly get any worse unless she began to parade naked in front of outsiders.

That, we agreed, would constitute insanity.

"Where is she now?" I asked.

"In her bedroom," Patricia replied. "She spends most of her time in there. Thank God!"

At that moment I heard footsteps upstairs.

"Oh Lord," said Patricia, stopping what she was doing and standing, frozen, completely still.

"I hope she realises that you're here already. What if she went into the sitting-room naked ... and found Eric ...? What on earth would he think?' said Patricia.

Patricia looked so pathetic and so silly and so hopelessly serious that I half wished Laurel would come downstairs naked and surprise Eric. I was suddenly infuriated by her absolute inability to have any control or influence over her children and her abject acceptance of their most idiotic stands. But I was in two minds. I hated the thought of Eric's salacious delight at the sight of Laurel.

All at once I heard a blood-curdling scream, and then pounding feet running across the hall. The kitchen door flew open and Laurel burst in. She was stark naked.

"There's an old man in the sitting-room," she yelled. And then on seeing me, "Oh, sorry, Aunt Prudence, I didn't realise you'd be here already." She turned and ran out of the room and when I next saw her at supper she was properly clothed.

In fact I suspect that as far as her earlier visit to the sitting-room was concerned, she had merely put her head round the door, seen Eric and run away. Anyway I am much too proud ever to question Eric over the matter, but I can hardly believe that, had he seen her in her full naked awfulness, he would have taken quite such a liking to her as he did.

To my amazement the evening passed quite smoothly, despite the fact that Victor, who was a little jumpy, had contrived the most peculiar blinkers in the form of large circles of cardboard wired to the sides of his spectacles and designed to prevent him from catching sight of Laurel out of the corner of his eye.

But while I talked to Victor, and Patricia dithered around waiting on us all, Eric distracted Laurel by talking to her all evening in the liveliest possible fashion. As for Laurel, I have never seen her so communicative nor so agreeable and, oddly enough, Eric did not appear to be in the least bit disconcerted by the child's peculiarly unappealing bald head.

He even said to me on the way home that although she would be an extremely pretty girl with hair, Laurel had such a fine skull that her baldness was hardly offensive at all. As for the idea that she was a little on the pudgy side, that didn't worry Eric either. He did not subscribe to the modern opinion that women should be all skin and bone. He liked to see a woman with good, old-fashioned curves.

I wondered if he had had too much to drink. After all he was referring to a mere child.

"No, no, my dear," he said, patting my knee in what was, I thought, a somewhat patronising manner, "I speak of women in general." Then he added, "A nice child." And after a pause, "It's all go."

Then Eric told me, as we drove on home, that he liked young people and that he had found Laurel especially appealing, frank, interesting and likeable.

That is not the impression which I usually have of my niece.

Eric appreciated her enquiring mind. She had expressed, he said, a great curiosity about Hinduism. Jesus had apparently let

79

her down badly recently and, as a result, she was thinking of abandoning her born-again Christianity in favour of a more meaningful religion.

I sighed. Poor Patricia, I thought.

Eric had some books on Hindu art which he had offered to show Laurel if she cared to come and see him, and she had promised to bicycle over at the weekend.

I gave Eric a sidelong glance. From what little I know of the matter, Hindu art is not a proper subject for perusal by an elderly man and a very silly adolescent girl.

By the time I had dropped Eric off at his house and returned home to find poor, abandoned Pansy welcoming me frantically after her long hours of solitude, I was quite exhausted. I fed my little dog who had indeed waited long enough, let her out for a run in the garden and finally fell exhausted into bed. It had been a long day and so much seemed to have happened. As I drifted into sleep I was haunted by a niggling feeling of unease. Was it Laurel? No, I didn't really care about her ... Perhaps it was the dancing ... that awful dancing in the garage ... me in my coat ... him in his mack ...

That was Tuesday. Today is Thursday and today, before I sat down and took out my pen, Eric telephoned. He was, I thought, in a ridiculous state of excitement.

"Your little niece rang," he said.

Little niece, my foot!

"Look Eric," I said rather sharply, "I'm afraid I'm busy. I'm writing you know." Suddenly I felt embarrassed, even by Eric. "I mean it's nothing important, and you would probably think it very silly — it is I know — but it helps me to sort out my thoughts. A diary you know. A memoir. Just a few things I want to get down."

I have no idea why I should have felt so apologetic towards Eric of all people. Perhaps I was just annoyed to be interrupted by thoughts of Laurel.

Laurel had telephoned Eric to confirm her intention of bicycling over to see him at the weekend.

And I had meant to spend this morning writing about Timothy.

Perhaps Eric put me off my stroke. Instead I seem to have dwelt in great detail on the events of the past few days.

*   *   *

In fact, after Leo came to see me at Blenkinsop's that Sunday afternoon, there were no new developments concerning Timothy for a long time.

The boy took to coming to see me as he had done before but rarely spoke of Leo. He did occasionally mention his mother, always with the same quality of bitterness and when I tried to draw him on the subject, thinking that it might relieve him to talk, he withdrew into himself. I could not help but suppose that Leo had something to do with Timothy's apparently ever increasing dislike of his mother.

Neither could I help the intense, caring feeling which I had for Timothy, and yet the closeness of the relationship which I felt I had with the child created an awkwardness and a tension around me which lasted throughout the term and which made me feel constantly nervous and as though I were under some kind of observation.

I will never understand what it was that lay at the root of this tension unless it was merely the foolish insensitivity of some of my colleagues who persisted in making the most futile allusions to my friendship with Timothy.

No doubt I loved Timothy a little more than I should have done under the circumstances, but to suggest that I was 'in love' with him was perfectly idiotic. Had I been 'in love' with one of my pupils, which would have been highly unlikely, I could not have allowed myself to see him as frequently as I saw Timothy, nor to invite him constantly to my house.

During the Easter holidays that year Timothy flew out to join his father who, with a new wife or mistress, had returned to Saudi Arabia. He did not want to go and I was saddened at the thought of his being so far away, but glad for him to be removed from the claustrophobic atmosphere of his mother and Leo.

Neither did I see Leo during those holidays and by the time

the school reassembled for the summer term I had begun to think that I had been allowing myself to get worked up over nothing and that I had become almost obsessional about Timothy.

But for some weeks my mind was turned to other things. I had been to London and to France with a colleague from the French department. I had redecorated my bedroom, tidied my small garden, prepared the remaining syllabus for the 'O' and 'A' level candidates, entertained Victor and Patricia for the night, visited a friend in hospital, been to the cinema, knitted a cardigan. Indeed I felt that I had altogether stopped thinking about Timothy and Leo, and Leo and Timothy and Mrs Hooper, and Mrs Hooper and Timothy. I could just look forward to the beginning of term with no undue feelings of discomfort.

And yet, as the first day of term drew near, I began to find myself wondering how Timothy had enjoyed staying with his father. I hoped that his father had been kind to him, for Timothy was a sensitive boy. I could not bear to think of him being hurt. I longed to know how he was, and I began to ask myself which were his favourite cakes. I hadn't made a cake for weeks. I checked my larder for the ingredients.

Yes. I was looking forward to seeing Timothy again. I had missed his lanky figure sprawled on my sofa. I had missed him sitting at my kitchen table eating bread and Marmite, his pale sensitive face, his green eyes, and I had missed his company. That was all.

He would soon be back.

CHAPTER
8

May 2nd

The Summer Term is always a busy one and that Summer Term was no exception. We in the staff room were naturally pre-occupied with the 'O' and 'A' level candidates, and there were athletics, and tennis matches, and concerts and plays and school outings to be organised as well. Everyone had something extra on their plate.

In the third week of term one of the French teachers fell ill and had to go into hospital which meant extra teaching all round for the rest of us. As a result I hardly had any time left over for poor Timothy although I was, as ever, conscious of his presence. He of course would not be sitting his 'O' levels until the following year when he would be sixteen.

Timothy had returned from Saudi Arabia looking taller, sun-tanned and healthy but he seemed to have withdrawn more than ever into his shell. He still came to see me, but not quite so often as before, partly, I suppose because I was so busy, but partly, no doubt, precisely because he was becoming more withdrawn.

I could not contemplate this withdrawal of his without a bitter twinge of fear. I felt that my friendship with Timothy was threatened, but I feared too for his sake. He was at a sensitive age, an age at which children can often crack up.

Or had I myself somehow offended him I wondered — given him cause to avoid me? I thought not. Perhaps he was quite simply bored with me. I truly hoped not. But there was no doubt about it that, even when he did come to see me, his conversations had become more stilted so that I was beginning to feel that I knew him less well rather than better than I had done before.

His work which had briefly improved under my tutelage seemed to have slackened off again and there were complaints about this from other members of the staff. There was no doubt about it. Timothy was not a happy boy.

I remembered with a pang the relaxed, friendly, out-of-school Timothy who had come to supper with me and Joan at Christmas time. How he had changed since then! And yet then it had seemed to me that we were on the brink of a very close friendship. Poor Timothy. It was sometimes almost as though I could feel the pain for him, but not knowing how to approach him, all I could do was to continue to invite him to tea and to hope that my house might at least provide some sort of a haven for him.

No doubt Timothy was upset by his parents and by his continued inability to find a niche for himself at school. I only wished with all my heart that I could somehow lessen the anguish for him. At times I would look at him and long to be able to put my arms around him and hug him. He looked like a young man crying out for the affection which his mother almost certainly never gave him.

Once as he sat at my kitchen table, his head dejectedly held in his hands, I stretched out my hand, almost inadvertently, to touch his thick golden hair. But I just withdrew it in time. Perhaps he would not have minded. I don't know. He was at that moment preoccupied with complaints about his housemaster.

It was during that Summer Term that I became convinced that, despite his earlier protestations, Leo had become the lover of Mrs Hooper. And I fear that he had done so for the sole purpose of getting nearer to Timothy.

Laughing, the two of them came to Blenkinsop's. Almost every other week. They swept around in that terrible motor-car. He at the wheel, she grimacing and gesticulating at his side. They never came to see me and when I happened to bump into them which I did on more than one occasion, Leo was embarrassed. He avoided catching my eye.

I was quite ashamed of Leo's behaviour and Timothy was no doubt ashamed of his mother's. The whole thing could not but create an awkwardness between us which partly, no doubt, explained Timothy's distancing himself from me.

Patricia told me on the telephone that Leo never bothered to come home any more. He hadn't even telephoned for weeks. She wondered if perhaps he had a girl-friend in London? Probably a fellow student. Had I heard anything from him?

No I hadn't. And indeed, I hadn't. I saw no reason for telling Patricia that although I had not heard from him, I had seen her son. She would have been horrified.

Once when Timothy came to tea, he complained very bitterly about the kind of people who steal other people's friends. Something really horrible ought to happen to them. I wondered if he were referring to his mother and Leo, he spoke with such feeling.

Timothy's housemaster remarked to me one day in the common-room that Mrs Hooper had been down again at the week-end, with her boy-friend.

"Looks more like some sort of a bloody queer than a gigolo to me," he said spitefully.

I supposed that he was unaware of the fact that he was speaking about my nephew. With a shameful feeling of treachery, I refrained from enlightening him.

Happily our conversation was interrupted by a member of the English staff, a man renowned throughout the school for his cultured refinement, not to mention the notorious passions with which he engulfed some of the better looking male pupils.

"I've decided on a production of *'Tis Pity She's a Whore* for next year's fifth form," he said. "Wharton would make a perfect Vasques."

I looked at him askance. Wharton was a particularly unintelligent Greek god of a rugger player. I doubted his ability to memorise even the smallest part.

"What a funny play to choose," I said, "for teenagers." And added, "What's wrong with Shakespeare?"

The English master gave me a withering glance.

"If we can't get up enough enthusiasm for *The Whore*," he said, "we'll do Beckett's *Endgame*."

"Not many parts for aspiring Thespians in that," I ventured.

As the bell rang for the end of break and the English master stalked away with his nose in the air, I wondered if the whole world were mad. What a ridiculous role *he* was playing.

As the term progressed I grew tenser and more anxious. Friends asked me repeatedly if I was unwell. I had lost weight and to a certain extent my appetite. I cannot explain, even now with hindsight, why it was that I felt so peculiarly unreal at that time. But then things which would formerly have seemed trivial took on an unwonted importance and other things which should have mattered to me, dwindled into insignificance.

An old friend's husband died of cancer. She rang me to tell me when the funeral would be. I remember spending hours poring over the road map to see if I could go to the funeral in Hemel Hempstead at midday and be back at school in time for Timothy's afternoon French lesson. Of course it wouldn't really matter if I missed that lesson, although I felt at the time that Timothy somehow needed someone, not so much to supervise him, as just to be around.

In the event I did miss Timothy's class that day. I had to go to the funeral and there was no way in which I could be back at Blenkinsop's by 3 o'clock.

At half term I went to stay with Victor and Patricia. I felt that I needed to get away from school although I am not sure that I was really right to go and stay with my brother.

Leo was there, moody and petulant, with purple hair. Patricia was out of her mind with anxiety about him, which seems strange now when I think of Laurel. Laurel at that time was a mere child. She must have been about eleven or twelve years old. Round and chubby and even quite appealing then.

Where, Patricia wanted to know, had she gone wrong, for her son to have done something so outrageous to his hair? She knew nothing then of green — of sage and privet and avocado and olive and apple . . .

The weekend was dull and, for me, fraught with tension.

I tried to talk to Leo but found him distracted and more than usually excitable. The only thing which I did learn from him, to my consternation, was that he was going to Corfu in July with Mrs Hooper and Timothy.

What on earth, I wondered, would Patricia and Victor think?

Leo, it appeared, had not told his parents and he begged me not to do so for him. That is to say that he had merely told them that he would be going away with friends. They, he presumed, supposed him to be going with fellow students.

Why, I asked him — perhaps with an element of malice — did he need to be so secretive?

He waved an airy-fairy hand in the air.

"They're not understanding," he said. "Not like you, dear auntie." And he looked at me intently with his large, trusting brown eyes.

I was flattered, of course, and it wasn't until later that it occurred to me that perhaps he only told me because he presumed that if Timothy hadn't already done so, he would be bound to do so soon.

When I got back to school, the whole place was in a fever of excitement as it always was when exams were about to start. But for all that, I could only think of Leo and Timothy and Mrs Hooper and Corfu. I could not bring myself to approve of that holiday plan at all and decided that I must broach the subject with Timothy before the end of term. He had, not surprisingly, refrained from mentioning the plan to me at all.

Just before the end of term Timothy came to call on me. He came unexpectedly and said that he would not have time to stay for tea. He shifted nervously from foot to foot and refused even to sit down. He picked at his hand and gazed almost shiftily at the floor. His golden hair fell across his brow. I sensed a tremendous tension. I don't think he really knew why he had come nor what it was that he wanted to say.

"I'm going home early," he eventually said. "Before the end of term." Then he paused.

I said nothing, waiting for him to speak again.

At last he said, "My mother's taking me to Corfu." He looked up at me quickly and then back at the floor. "It's terribly embarrass-ing."

I wondered how he had managed to get permission to leave school early. The headmaster was usually most particular about pupils staying until the very end of term.

Timothy's mother was not one to kow-tow to headmasters. She would just come down and fetch him.

I looked at him sharply. I supposed that that meant that Leo would just come down with her to fetch him.

Timothy blushed.

"I've told you what I think about my mother," he said. "Well, I hate Leo too, if you want to know. He goes to bed with her." He paused. "With my mother."

I was dreadfully embarrassed.

'Oh Timothy, my dear," I said lamely, "I'm sure you've imagined it."

"That is not the sort of thing I go about imagining," he said with amazing ferocity, and burst into tears, sinking as he did so onto the sofa.

It hurt me to see him there, half man, half child, his head sunk in despair, tears rolling down his pale cheeks, his shoulders heaving. This time I went to him, put my arms around him and held him closely to me. His flesh smelt of sweet sweat, but I didn't mind. I went on cradling his head and God alone knows when I would have stopped if the telephone hadn't rung.

I turned to answer it – it was a wrong number – and when I turned back, Timothy had stood up, stopped crying and was blowing his nose on a rather grubby looking paper handkerchief.

"I'm terribly sorry," he said. "It's just that they both make me sick and I've got to go away with them. And if you must know, I think your nephew's a poof. I wish I'd never met him."

I felt appallingly guilty, but then I could hardly have imagined such an outcome when I originally introduced Leo to Timothy. I had only wanted to be kind then. I still only wanted to be kind.

Really I had no idea what to say. I had never been in such a situation in my life before.

"Have a cup of tea," I said, "and let's talk things over." I was sure that we would both feel better after a good talk.

But Timothy had said enough. He didn't want to talk about it any more. He had to go. He would see me next term.

As he left I felt my heart contract in a feeling of inexplicable fear. I had done nothing to help him and it would be a very long time before I saw him again. He would change during the summer holidays; he would be sixteen by the time he came back, or very nearly — quite a young man. Suddenly it crossed my mind that he might not come back at all. I didn't know why he shouldn't but everything about Timothy seemed so desperate and so uncertain that I had no idea what to expect.

Those holidays lasted for an eternity. Unusually I had made no plans to go away and so was stuck in my house, right next to the school, for the whole of the summer. I spent most of my time gardening or walking Pansy although I did occasionally arrange to see friends, but so much of my concentration was devoted to worrying about Timothy and Leo and Corfu that I must have been poor company.

I longed for the Autumn Term and yet I dreaded it for I was terrified of learning that Timothy had left to continue his education elsewhere. He was so unhappy at school that it seemed quite possible to me that he might persuade his parents to take him away. Of course it would be a great mistake if they did — right in the middle of the 'O' level syllabus.

So I could almost say that it was with relief that I saw the Porsche sweep into the school drive on the first day of term. Leo was still at the wheel with Mrs Hooper beside him and Timothy, more or less in hiding, behind. I happened to be walking down the drive at the time, on my way to fetch some books which I had left at home. For one reason or another I seem to have spent a great deal of that afternoon walking up and down the drive.

I do not know whether Leo saw me, but I can only suppose that he must have done. In any case I hardly need say that he did not come to call on me that day.

But he did come later in the term.

*　　*　　*

Eric's opera-going lady friend came to stay with him for the week-end. I, of course, was eaten up with curiosity and longed to meet her. I suggested that he bring her over for a drink before lunch on Sunday, but he made some inadequate excuse. Perhaps, like me, he feels the need to keep his life compartmentalised.

He did, however, reveal that his friend had had a very sad life. Her only child, a little girl, had died of leukaemia at the age of nine. A painful expression crossed Eric's face as he told me about it. He stared distractedly into the distance and drummed his fingers on the arm of the chair.

"She was very cut up at the time," he said. "Very cut up."

So, I thought, the opera-going lady was not like me, a spinster. She must be a widow or a divorcee. But I dared ask no more.

"She'll be wanting a quiet week-end," he said. "She works very hard."

Ah . . . so she still works, I thought. She must be younger than us.

"What does she do?" I ventured.

"She's a chiropodist," he said.

I nearly laughed.

"Anyway, I must be getting on," he said, heaving himself out of the chair. "All this chat is getting us nowhere."

I saw him to the door and watched him shuffle off down the path, leaving me with a faint feeling of pique . . . almost loneliness.

On Sunday morning I was walking back from church when Eric drove by. I just caught a glimpse of the woman sitting beside him in the front of the car. She looked neat and pretty and, as far as I could tell from that distance, quite young. Somewhere in her mid-fifties perhaps.

I thought that I had long since learned to live with the appearance which the good Lord gave me, but, to my horror, I felt a faint resurgence of that old, self-pitying melancholy which used to well up in me years ago whenever I saw a particularly pretty and feminine woman.

How absurd I am, I thought. Eric is nothing to me. Just a

companion, a companion who, through his own loneliness has sought me out, and with whom I pass some pleasant times. It would be quite absurd to resent his other friends. Indeed, it would be a very peculiar thing if he had none. And yet I wondered where they were going to in that car.

Perhaps he was taking her to Porlock or Lynton ... or Isle Abbots ... It occurred to me that she could hardly be expected to find the week-end restful if she was to spend it hurtling about the countryside in Eric's shaky old car.

Ah well, that was none of my business.

What I consider to be much more my business is Eric's swiftly developing relationship with my niece, Laurel.

Eric's repeatedly uttered clichés certainly belie his character which has an undoubtedly reckless streak.

Not content with the company of a pretty chiropodist throughout the week-end, Eric entertained Laurel to lunch yesterday. Yesterday was Monday, and I dearly wanted to know why Laurel was not at school.

Because of his lady friend, Eric had asked Laurel not to come at the week-end. She had happily agreed to come on Monday instead.

"Do her parents know she's coming to lunch with you, instead of going to school?" I asked him on the telephone.

"I've no idea," he said.

It is not part of my nature ever to cause trouble if I can avoid it, so I decided that rather than speak to Patricia, or even Victor, about the matter, I would look in on Eric immediately after lunch on the pretext of wanting to borrow something. That way Laurel would know that I knew what she was up to and, what is more, I would be able to ask her why she wasn't at school.

The sun was shining yesterday and the birds were singing so I spent most of the morning weeding my garden. My white lilac is coming into bloom and there are Kaufmaniana tulips and sweet smelling Daphne so that it is all beginning to look really pretty — or it was until this morning when the heavens opened. I woke to the sound of rain at about six and now it is nearly one o'clock and as I look out of the window I can see my poor lilac bending under the great weight of the water, and it is still raining.

Well at about this time yesterday I was just collecting up my secateurs and trowel and so forth and thinking that I had done enough for one morning, when I heard the sound of a scooter and looked up to see Laurel in shorts and a bright red T-shirt whizzing past on her way to visit Eric.

She was easily identifiable as, to my horror, she was riding without her crash helmet, the silly child. And with that bald head, she is quite unmistakeable.

I decided to wait for about fifty-five minutes to give her and Eric time to have lunch before going round to call. But call I certainly would.

I have to admit that when I turned up, almost exactly fifty minutes later, neither Eric nor Laurel appeared best pleased to see me.

The back door was open, so I wandered in unannounced and there they were, sitting side by side at Eric's kitchen table, surrounded, like a pair of students, by dirty plates and mugs of coffee, and poring over a book which lay open on the table between them. Laurel was smoking a cigarette.

As I came in they both started, and turned to look at me. I couldn't help thinking that they made rather a funny couple. He with his still thick, woolly grey hair, and lined, tired face, she with her shiny, bald head and smooth round face. As they looked up, they both wore an expression of marginally irritated surprise.

Eric was the first to collect himself.

"Oh Prudence," he said, and stood up, "come on in. Have some coffee. You know Laurel . . ." He waved a hand in her direction and shuffled his feet awkwardly.

"Of course you do. How silly of me," he said, and blushed I think, as he moved towards the kettle.

Laurel said "Hello" rather sourly and I felt, I have to admit, a little discomfited, like an intruder.

"What, not at school, Laurel dear," I said and raised one eyebrow.

"It's not worth it," said Laurel. "They spend all the time on useless revision classes."

"Revision is never useless," I said. After all I have not been a school-mistress all my life for nothing.

"It is, the way they do it," she said rudely.

There was no point in continuing to argue and neither did I want to embarrass Eric but I did just enquire if Patricia knew where Laurel was.

"She didn't ask," said Laurel and turned her gaze on the open book in front of her as Eric handed me a cup of Nescafé.

Of course I know that as Patricia's children seem to do precisely what they want, it is not really relevant whether or not she knows where they are. But I do think it is a good thing for Laurel to realise that I have my eye on her.

"Eric," she said, impertinently calling him by his Christian name, "asked me here to discuss Hindu art. He knows a lot about it."

That was news to me.

"I don't think Aunt Prudence would like this kind of thing very much, do you," she said, turning to Eric with a sweet smile and pointing to a picture which I could not see from that distance and which, anyway, would have been upside down for me.

I was so incensed by the child's impudence that I got up and left almost instantly, without finishing my coffee or mentioning the crash helmet and having quite forgotten to ask to borrow some slug pellets, an excuse which I had devised for calling.

Now, with all this rain, whole armies of slugs will be on the march and I have no pellets with which to confound them. Perhaps I shall go out and buy some this afternoon.

As for Eric, I must have a word with him about Laurel. He is surely old enough to know better, and has no business encouraging that silly girl to smoke cigarettes and to miss school.

CHAPTER
9

Eric came to see me this morning, looking, I thought, a little apologetic. I hadn't seen him since the beginning of the week when I interrupted his lunch with Laurel. For some reason which I can't quite explain to myself, the memory of that incident leaves me feeling a little uncomfortable. Perhaps it is because of that that I have failed to ring Eric about Laurel, as I had every intention of doing.

I told Eric, somewhat inhospitably, that I was delighted to see him as the washer on my kitchen tap needed replacing.

He smiled, rather wryly I thought, and set obediently to work.

Which of us, I wondered, would be the first to raise the subject of Laurel. He, perhaps, would attempt to avoid the subject altogether. Men, I have observed even without having been married to one, are past masters of non-confrontation. They even seem to think that if they don't want a subject to be discussed, they can, by sheer determination, prevent other people from so much as thinking about it.

So I said nothing for a while as Eric chatted about this and that, about the quality of washers nowadays and about the bad weather we have been having all week.

"Except for Monday," I said. "It was lovely the day Laurel came to see you . . ." I paused.

"The seeds will be rotting in the ground, it's so wet," Eric said. "I shan't have many vegetables this year."

"There you are," he said, putting the wrench down on the

94

draining board and turning the tap on and off again, "that should be all right."

I thanked him and then added in what sounded, even to me, like regrettably school-mistressy tones, "I think we should have a word about Laurel."

Then Eric took me completely by surprise.

He looked me straight in the eye and said, "You needn't worry. I have no intention of running away with her. In any case, I don't suppose she'd come, although they say it's better to be an old man's darling . . ." he chortled somehow privately to himself and annoyed me. "I won't even take her dancing in a petrol station," he added as he sat down at my kitchen table.

I felt myself blushing foolishly.

"Come on," he said, "aren't you going to offer me a cup of coffee?"

I had never known him so assertive.

"Of course I am," I said, and went on lamely, "It's just that I don't think Laurel should be encouraged to miss school, and you know her parents don't allow her to smoke. I wouldn't let her smoke here."

That was quite understandable, but Eric was an outsider, not a parent nor an uncle, He was in no position to tell Laurel whether or not she could smoke. Of course it was a shame that she did. But there you were.

"You don't want to worry about Laurel," he said. "She'll be all right when she gets rid of some of her silly ideas." Then, suddenly confiding, "I would love to have a daughter, you know."

I looked askance at Eric. Was he, I wondered, being completely honest with himself? It doesn't seem to me that his attitude to Laurel is entirely paternal although the idea that it could be anything else amazes me.

"She wants to go to Glastonbury and Cadbury," he said. "She's interested in Arthurian legends."

I can't help noticing that Laurel has suddenly developed a great many surprising interests about which I have never heard before, what with Hindu art and now Arthurian legends.

"I would have thought that she must at least have been to Glastonbury before now," I said.

"No, she's never been there," said Eric. "I thought we might take her one day. You and I together. We could go on to South Cadbury, although I'm told that's a little disappointing and not at all what one would imagine for Camelot."

I am not sure that the idea of Laurel intruding on my outings with Eric is entirely pleasing to me. I have begun to enjoy those outings most particularly for Eric is a good and likeable companion who takes tremendous pleasure in whatever it is that he's doing, and this enjoyment enthuses me.

How I hated dancing with him in that dreadful petrol station, but the more I think about that incident, the more I feel some strange sort of respect for Eric. I am, and always have been, inhibited – prudent I have called it – but he, who is so perfectly mannered and who always speaks in clichés which for months made me think of him as a really dull man, is able to break out suddenly and take the world – or his small world at least – by surprise. I suppose that I have never in my entire life taken anyone by surprise.

If I am to be perfectly honest with myself, I have to admit that I look forward to my outings with Eric as much as I look forward to anything these days. It may be a strange thing to say at my time of life, but I think – in fact I know – that I have never before experienced such an easy and companionable relationship with a person of the opposite sex. I could pity myself for what I have missed in that field, but I try to look at life positively and so I tell myself how lucky I am to have so pleasant a friendship develop in later life.

So now Laurel is to intrude on that friendship. I could hardly refuse to take my own niece to Camelot, besides which it seems far more suitable to me that I should be present if Eric is to take the child on long outings. So I agreed to go on the trip to Glastonbury which is to take place next Saturday, but I have to say that I do hope that we are not about to become a permanent, awkward threesome.

I didn't see Eric again until Saturday afternoon when he passed by in his car to pick me up. I had been watching for him from my window and as I walked down my garden path, I did not at first recognise the girl sitting beside him in the passenger seat. She had long, peculiarly fuzzy, reddish hair and, as I approached, she jumped out of the car.

"Aunt Prudence," she said, "you get in front, I'll go behind."

I did what can only be described, I believe, as a 'double take'.

How extraordinary!

"Where did you get all that hair from, so suddenly?" I asked.

"It's a wig," said Laurel and pulled the frizzy, synthetic mess away from her head to reveal three days growth on her otherwise bald pate.

"Put it back on!" I explained shrilly. And I am happy to say that she did.

"I had to have hair to go to Camelot," she said. "Don't you think so?"

I told her that as far as I was concerned she was better off with hair wherever she went. Camelot was neither here nor there.

All the way to Glastonbury Laurel chattered away in the back of the car. I sat in the front with Pansy on my knee, barely able to hear a word that she was saying and intensely irritated by her hot breath in my ear and by the occasional brush of nylon fluff across my cheek as she leaned her head between the two front seats so as to be heard more clearly.

Eric, on the other hand, drove along with what I regarded as an irritating smirk on his face. I could not understand why he was so delighted. Laurel's conversation seemed to me to be perfectly idiotic. For one thing she appeared to have no understanding whatsoever of the nature of a legend so that she persisted in talking about Lancelot and Gawain and Guinevere not even as though they were real, historical characters, but as if they were her school friends whom she saw every day.

At Glastonbury I felt a little embarrassed by Laurel and, at the same time, ashamed to be embarrassed by her. After all there are plenty of odd-looking young people around these days and, anyway, I should have reached an age when I am beyond such childish discomfort. But, all the same, I did feel rather ill at ease, accompanied, as I was, by an elderly man and a fat teenager in a hideous wig. In fact it was not until we got out of the car at Glastonbury that I quite took in how Laurel was dressed. Besides her horrid wig, she was wearing a long white nightdress with some kind of fluorescent turquoise binder-twine wrapped around her body so that she looked like an ill-conceived parcel although, she assured me later, the object of the exercise was to look medieval.

She walked along beside Eric, chatting in a lively fashion, always about Gawain and Guinevere and he kept on smirking and smirking and smiling inanely, And I walked with Pansy several steps behind.

When we had visited the ruins of the Abbey, we walked up to the Tor, and still Laurel talked, and still Eric smirked, and still I walked behind, and then, somewhat exhausted, we climbed back into the car and set out for South Cadbury, about half an hour's drive away.

By the time we reached South Cadbury, Laurel was in a fever of excitement. I have no idea what it was that she really expected to see. Turrets and battlements, and knights in armour and ladies in wimples and Sir Lancelot singing Tirra-lirra by the river, no doubt.

Whatever, she must have been disappointed.

We trudged up a stony path through messy unkempt woodland to a dull green field where a few mangy cattle grazed. We wandered to the edge of the field, hoping to look down on some magical, poetic landscape, but there was little to delight the eye.

Eric had thrown out his arms theatrically, but overcome by the uninspiring nature of the place, he let them drop to his side as he turned back towards Laurel.

"Let's face it," he said, "it's not quite the Camelot we imagined."

A group of school children accompanied by two teachers had materialised from nowhere to stare balefully at us.

Then quite unexpectedly, Eric flung out his arms again.

> "'Enid,'" he cried, "'the pilot star of my lone life,
> 'Enid, my early and my only love,
> 'Enid, the loss of whom hath turned me wild . . .'"

Turned him wild indeed.

Laurel for some reason decided then to execute a little dance and before I knew what was happening, she too began to declaim.

> "'And Enid answer'd, 'Yea, my lord, I know
> 'Your wish, and would obey; but riding first,
> 'I hear the violent threats you do not hear,
> 'I see the danger which you cannot see . . .'"

I stood awkwardly by. The school children gawped and giggled. The school teachers stared in blank amazement. There was no stopping them now. Eric was off again, his woolly hair standing on end, his eyes flashing.

> "'With that he turn'd and look'd as keenly at her
> 'As careful robins eye the delver's toil . . .'"

And Laurel took up the strain:

> "'And that within her, which a wanton fool
> 'Or hasty judger would have called her guilt,
> 'Made her cheek turn and either eyelid fall.
> 'And Geraint looked and was not satisfied . . .'"

I thought they would go on for ever, but eventually they grew tired of what they were doing, thank God, or perhaps they just ran out of lines which they knew by heart.

Eric's arms dropped to his sides again and he shuffled over towards me. His cheeks were flushed and his hair was still sticking up all over his head.

"Smoothe your hair down," I said.

He smoothed his hair ineffectually with one hand, whilst placing the other on my shoulder.

"Poor Prudence," he said, "I'm always embarrassing you." He

turned to look at Laurel. "Sometimes I take your aunt by surprise," he said. "Ah well, it's a funny old world."

Funny indeed. Laurel looked quite crazy standing there all tied up in binder twine with her orange wig askew. But she, too, had taken me by surprise. In fact, I have been seeing quite a new and unexpected side to Laurel lately. I suppose that I have never until now ever seen her without her parents. And heaven only knows what they would have said had they heard her declaiming at Camelot.

"I can't imagine what those other people must have thought about you two," I said rather primly.

As soon as the performance had ended, the school party had wandered off and disappeared almost as suddenly as it had appeared.

"Who cares what they thought?" said Laurel. "Anyway, we probably livened up their outing for them."

I had reluctantly to concede that she was probably right.

By the time we had all three climbed back into the car, I was quite exhausted, but Laurel, who was still full of life, talked and talked all the way home, pushing her face between the two front seats as she had done on the way out, so I was really glad when Eric at last drew up in front of my cottage and too tired even to ask him and Laurel in for a cup of tea. I sincerely hope that Laurel will not be included on our next trip. She is a tiring child who demands a great deal of attention. Thank the Lord there are no Hindu temples in the vicinity. Camelot was bad enough.

As soon as Pansy and I were indoors, I sank down onto my sofa without even bothering to take off my coat. I felt a strange emptiness, almost a sense of desolation. I wondered how many more years I had to live and I wished that Eric would look in for supper. But I supposed he wouldn't. Perhaps he had invited Laurel to have supper with him and perhaps they were, at that very moment, poring over pictures of indecent Hindu carvings. I could see Laurel's fuzzy red wig brushing Eric's cheek as she talked and pointed and gesticulated. And I could imagine Eric grinning idiotically beside her. Silly man. Or perhaps Laurel had taken her wig off again. Perhaps she didn't need it for Hindu art.

Lately I have been so concerned with Eric and Laurel and the garden and Pansy who has had to go to the vet about an eye infection, that I have quite put Timothy out of my mind.

Sometimes Timothy and his problems seem so far away and at other times, I sit and think about him and wonder how he is now and what he is up to and whether I will ever see him again, and then it seems like only yesterday that he was eating crumpets and cake in my old kitchen.

Of course he is quite grown-up now, and no doubt very good looking.

It is true that I was really relieved to see Timothy back at school after those summer holidays although he seemed definitely to have grown even further away from me. At first I put this down to the awkwardness he must feel at having told me about his mother and Leo, and to the discomfort of having been on holiday with them both. Naturally I was dying of curiosity about that holiday and hoped very much that Timothy would soon come round to tea and tell me all about it.

In fact Timothy did not come to see me for about three weeks by which time I was beginning to be seriously worried about him. In his French lessons he sat silently at the back of the class, rarely raising his eyes from the desk in front of him. He exchanged as few words as possible, certainly with me, and as far as I could see, with everyone else as well.

He walked about the school with his shirt tails hanging out and his shoelaces untied. He looked scruffy and dejected and vacant. His work was nearly always handed in late and was of poor quality when it appeared. His housemaster had had words with him and even he, for all his insensitivity, wondered if the boy were worried about something or if he were just suffering from what he called typical schoolboy indolence and bloody-mindedness.

Once or twice I had suggested that Timothy might look in for tea, but he had not turned up. I decided that the time had come for me to bring authority to bear. I would tell him that I wished to speak to him about his work. Then he would have to come.

So on the Friday of the third week of term Timothy came to my house at five o'clock in the afternoon. I had not baked a cake.

"I asked you here," I told him rather curtly, "to talk about your work."

He stared at the floor.

I told him strictly how important it was for him to work. I said all the things which school teachers say to children. I told him that he was letting himself down; I asked him to think of the future; I told him that he must learn to grow up and I told him that he was letting down his parents who, after all, were spending a great deal of money to give him a good education and that he might regret the wasted opportunities for the rest of his life.

He waited patiently for me to finish and then looked up and stared me straight in the eyes.

"Don't talk about my parents," he said. "You know what I think of them. Of my mother anyway." He looked at the ground again.

"The holidays were foul," he went on. "Sometimes I just wish I were dead." And then he said, looking at me again, "Have you ever wished you were dead? Have you ever walked to the edge of a cliff and looked over, and wished you had the courage to jump?"

My blood froze.

"Timothy," I said, "you mustn't, you really mustn't talk like that." I had stretched out my hand to touch him and was holding him firmly by the wrist.

"Don't worry," he said, "I don't suppose I'd ever dare."

Of course I was worried. I was worried sick.

"I'll make some tea," I said. "You'll find some biscuits in the cupboard. I'm afraid," I added, lamely apologising, "I haven't made a cake today." I wished I had.

"You've always been kind to me," he said stiffly, "and I am very grateful."

I felt my eyes pricking and turned away to pour the boiling water into the pot.

Timothy stayed with me for a long time that day. He missed evening prep but I was in a position to see that he wouldn't get into trouble about that.

For the first time since I had known him, Timothy talked a great deal about himself. Once he had started it was almost as if nothing would stop him.

He told me how lonely he was and how pointless everything was. Sometimes he would sit down in his room or in the library with every intention of doing some work, but he would soon find himself staring vacantly out of the window or at the floor, or sometimes he would fall into a deep sleep and wake hours later still feeling exhausted with nothing achieved. He didn't know why, but he just seemed quite unable to make himself work. He had even stopped writing poetry.

He used to think that things would be better when he left school, but then he wasn't really looking forward to that either because he didn't know what he would do. He didn't want to go to university and he didn't want to be shut up in an office all day, he didn't want to join the army and anyway he didn't have any particular talents.

In some ways school, which was hell, was better than home. Home meant either Jeddah which he hated, a father with whom he appeared to have little understanding and his father's mistress whom he didn't like at all, or it meant his mother and Leo. Leo was still always hanging around his mother and it made him sick.

Leo made him sick. Couldn't his mother see that Leo was much more interested in Timothy than in her?

And Leo wouldn't take 'no' for an answer. He was forever pestering Timothy.

I didn't care to go into the details of what that pestering might entail, but I decided that at the very next possible opportunity I would have to have a word with Leo. It would be both difficult and embarrassing but I must do it. Had I not just heard a young boy talking of death and suicide? Indeed I could not wait for an opportunity to present itself, I would have to make a point of seeing Leo.

When Timothy eventually left me that evening, I felt that

although talking must have helped him, he was in a very bad way indeed. Apart from confronting Leo, I was not sure what the best course of action might be. Timothy had promised me that he would try to work, but I could hardly see how he was going to be able to change his ways overnight. He also promised to come and see me on a regular basis. He needed, I felt sure, to be in everyday, fairly close contact with somebody, and that contact was at least something which I could offer.

So for the next few weeks I did see Timothy regularly. He came to see me two or three times a week, if not more, and I made biscuits and baked cakes for him and listened to his troubles which seemed to go round and round in circles and which were apparently insoluble. The only solution that I could see to them lay in his being able to make himself work. But the ability to work continued to elude him. I was beginning to grow desperate on his behalf and on his behalf I felt tense and nervous; and because of him I became abstracted and found difficulty, myself, in concentrating on my work.

All my emotions and all my thoughts were involved in caring for that boy. For the first time I began fully to understand the desperation of a mother with an unhappy, difficult child.

I tried to contact Leo, but with little success. He never answered my letters and when I rang Patricia she said that he hadn't been in touch for a long time. She had almost begun to wonder whether she still had a son. But, on the whole, it was better for Leo not to come home. Victor was quite put out with him and if he did come, Patricia was sure the atmosphere would be most uncomfortable. She sometimes envied me for having no children.

"You can have no idea, Prudence," she said, "how lucky you are . . ."

I thought of poor Timothy and sighed. She couldn't conceivably love Leo more than I loved Timothy. She certainly didn't care for him so much.

"If you do hear from Leo, please ask him to get in touch with me as soon as possible," I said.

Patricia appeared to have no curiosity as to why I wanted to speak to her son, which was just as well.

In the event I had to wait a few more weeks before he suddenly turned up at Blenkinsop's, without Mrs Hooper this time, and came to call on me.

During those weeks something of great importance had occurred. Natalie had appeared on the scene.

CHAPTER
10

May 28th

Natalie had been at Blenkinsop's for as long as Timothy and although I had never taught her, I was, like every other member of staff, aware of her presence in the school, mainly because her name was all too frequently among those on the detention list which was pinned up in the staff room regularly at the end of every week. She was a small, dumpy child with a round face and straight mousy hair. From her appearance no one would have supposed her to be a naughty girl and yet she was for ever in trouble. She skipped lessons, failed to hand in her work, climbed out of school at night, answered the teachers back, was flagrantly disobedient, played practical jokes, smoked, probably drank, raised petitions for the sacking of the headmaster and generally made a nuisance of herself. She was usually to be seen leading a gang of silly, admiring girls around the school. Girls who obeyed her every command.

It seemed to me that Natalie walked on very thin ice indeed and I was often amazed that, if the stories one heard about her were true, the headmaster was prepared to tolerate her in the school at all. I imagined that he did not in fact expel her because she was very clever. Oxbridge material. She would one day bring honour to the school. She would win a scholarship — or at least an exhibition — to Balliol and her name would go up in gold letters at Blenkinsop's, a school which was hardly famed for its academic success, and all her misdeeds would then be forgotten.

When Natalie returned to school that Autumn Term, there

was more than the usual amount of talk about her in the staff common room.

"Have you seen Natalie Knight this term?" a lugubrious chemistry teacher enquired. He was looking rather less lugubrious than usual. "She's changed completely during the holidays."

Indeed she had. She had changed so much that some of us even failed to recognise her at first. For one thing she had shot up. She must have grown at least two inches and in doing so, she had slimmed down. She even had quite a pretty figure. Her face seemed less round, her neck longer, her nose bigger, and her mousy hair had been given a vivid henna rinse. It stood on end and shone, a luminous, purplish red. She had plucked her eyebrows to two fine arches and her large, light brown eyes were coated with purple and blue mascara. A pair of very large gold rings hung from her ears. Those, of course, were not allowed at Blenkinsop's but that would hardly have bothered Natalie.

There was no doubt about it, Natalie Knight had, during the course of one summer holiday, turned from an ugly duckling into a lovely young swan.

"There's hope for us all," said the lugubrious chemistry teacher.

I glanced at his bald head and the bags under his eyes and wondered what chance he had at so late a stage of turning into a swan. He must have been sixty if he was a day.

The first time I saw Natalie and Timothy together, I caught sight of them walking through the town one Saturday afternoon. I have to admit that I was quite surprised. They seemed to me to be a most unlikely couple at the best of times, and I could not for the life of me imagine what had brought them together. I was further amazed by the fact that they appeared to be deep in conversation.

I do not think that either of them spotted me on that occasion. In any case I, not wishing to meet them, crossed the road and disappeared into a shop. It would be perfectly true to say that since I had grown so fond of Timothy, he was never at the best of times far from my mind, but ever since he had spoken to me of his despair, I had found it very difficult to think of anything else or anyone else at all. I spent hours worrying about him and his plight. I thought of him first thing in the morning and last thing at night. If I woke in the small hours, I thought of him then. I prayed for him in church, watched for him in school and counted the days and indeed the hours until he was due to visit me again.

He did come, as he had promised to do, regularly and although he never spoke again so explicitly of his despair, I could feel the weight of his depression in his languid movements and in the dull stare of his green eyes. I tried my best to give him hope, even to bring a smile to his sad face but it seemed as though it were beyond my powers.

It was inconceivable, I thought as I grilled a kipper for my supper that Saturday evening, quite inconceivable that Timothy could have taken a fancy to Natalie. I felt my heart constrict with fear. That would be a dreadful thing. Natalie could be nothing but a bad influence on Timothy. There must be some other explanation for their having walked into the town together.

I went to cut a slice of bread to make some toast. The loaf of bread reminded me of Timothy. It was white. I used always to buy wholemeal bread, but since Timothy had expressed a marked preference for white bread I had taken to buying that for his tea and now I too preferred it.

It was not just the white bread that reminded me of Timothy. As time went by more and more things had begun to remind me of him every day. Place names, like Ashford in Kent where he once casually mentioned that his aunt lived; Burton-on-Trent where he happened to have told me his father was born; London, Jeddah, Saudi Arabia, Mecca, Hampstead where his grandparents lived. Any mention of the colour green made me think of his eyes, fast cars made me think of him, the smell of a cake cooking, the smell of the school corridors, any reference to Christmas, to exams, to French lessons, to loneliness, laziness, beauty, despair . . .

I began to realise that I was in danger of becoming obsessional, and yet it was hardly surprising that the boy should be on my mind. After all I was probably the only person who had really cared for him at all over the last two years and now he was in a state of near suicidal despair which was not likely to be helped by an association with a naughty little flibbertigibbet.

Leo, too, in a way, had cared for Timothy. That I had to admit. But I was not sure that I particularly approved of his method of caring although it entered my head then to turn to Leo for advice.

By the time I had eaten my kipper and cleared away my plate, I was still thinking about Timothy and turning over in my mind what to do about him. Perhaps there was nothing to his being seen with Natalie and yet the very thought of Natalie caused my heart to constrict and a wave of awful dread to sweep through me.

I went to fetch a pile of books which needed correcting in the hope that they at least would take my mind off the problem.

The very next morning as I entered the staff common-room I heard the odious voice of Timothy's housemaster.

"Good-morning to you, Prudence." There was a hint of insolence in his tone.

"Good-morning, James," I said calmly.

"I hear your little toy-boy's going out" (his vowel sounds left much to be desired) "with the naughtiest girl in the school."

How I hated that man. I felt the blush which suffused me spreading over my entire body so that I should not have been surprised to find that even my knees had turned pink.

"A little rivalry, my dear Prudence," he said, "that's all," and put his great, square, freckled hand on my shoulder.

I shrugged it off and said angrily, "Can't you stop being so silly." Tears of confusion pricked behind my eyelids.

"Oh come on Prudence, don't take it so seriously. You know I'm only teasing," said James, and added almost kindly, "After all the boy should be grateful to you. You've been bloody good to him."

"I just worry about him, that's all," I said tensely.

"I only hope this love affair — if that's what you like to call it — won't get the boy into a bigger mess than he's in already," he said, and then left me to talk to a pretty young history mistress who had joined the school that term and whose private life was a constant source of interest to those members of staff most concerned with tittle-tattle — indeed to the school as a whole. Some said that she was a lesbian, others that she was having an affair with a sixth form boy. I listened to none of it, but was infinitely grateful to her on that morning for diverting the attention of Timothy's horrible housemaster.

From that day on I began to notice that Timothy was to be seen everywhere in the company of Natalie who had abandoned her gaggle of acolytes in his favour.

I have to admit that he looked happier with her than he had done mooching around the school all alone. He and Natalie seemed to be permanently engrossed in conversation as they went about hand-in-hand, in blatant defiance of the six — or was it ten inch — rule. I cannot to this day imagine what they found to talk about.

Timothy's appearance changed at about the same time as he began to be seen with Natalie. He took to using some sort of gel on his hair so that it stood up in spikes all over his head, and he even walked with something of a swagger. This, one might think, was all very well, but his work did not improve. In fact I would go so far as to say that it actually deteriorated, if that was conceivably possible. To be more precise, he started to skip lessons, a crime which I regarded with the greatest concern. What on earth, I wondered, would become of the boy. I was worried sick.

I hardly need add that Timothy had stopped coming to see me. Indeed he seemed to avoid me.

It was imperative, I decided, that I speak to Leo. He might have some influence on Timothy, although, when I think of it now I cannot imagine why I thought such a thing since Timothy had declared his ardent dislike of Leo to me. But then I was at my wits' end. Here was a desperate boy, momentarily infatuated with a hopelessly silly girl, taking every day, one way or another, a further step towards self-destruction. And here was I, apparently the only person who cared for him, quite unable to approach him and completely lost.

At one stage I thought of having a word with Natalie herself, but I knew the sort of girl she was. She would have tossed her head in rude disdain, probably even told me to mind my own business and then, to add insult to injury, she would have laughed behind my back and boasted of her own impertinence, even made fun of me to Timothy. One thing I could not bear was to think of Timothy laughing at me.

I wrote to Leo, but again, he did not reply. I was desperate.

Then about three quarters of the way through term, by which time not only Timothy but Natalie, too, were running into serious trouble, Leo suddenly telephoned me. He wanted to see me. I was both amazed and glad. He arranged to come down the following Saturday. He would come alone, he said, and would like to stay the night. I was delighted.

*　　　*　　　*

On Tuesday morning I looked out of the window. It was a beautiful sunny day and Eric was ambling up the garden path. I watched him from behind the curtain. He couldn't see me, I was sure. Suddenly he turned and stepped on to the lawn, and stood quite still, staring intently in the direction of a group of shrubs.

I went on watching him for a while, wondering what it was that so absorbed his attention. It occurred to me that he looked quite charming, standing there engrossed in his own private world, unaware of being observed. He was nice looking and from where I was I could not see if he had done up his fly-buttons or not. Then, all at once, I felt ashamed of the spiteful way I laughed to myself about his inadequacies. Perhaps I, too, was prone to the weaknesses of age. Never mind his fly-buttons, he had a good, strong profile and a gentle expression on his tired face. If we were younger, perhaps I could have fallen in love with him. Perish the thought.

Perish the thought indeed, for no sooner had it crossed my mind than I realised that age is of no account. My guard was down and as I gazed unseen at Eric standing alone in my sunny garden, I suddenly felt intensely excited and young again. Oh dear, oh dear. I also felt rather foolish.

As I watched him Eric turned back onto the path and walked towards the front door. I moved quickly away from the window for fear of being seen and went to let him in.

I suppose that as I opened the door I must have been smiling broadly.

"You're looking very well this morning," Eric said brightly.

"So are you," I replied with unaccustomed warmth. "What were you looking at in the garden?"

"You've a pair of greenfinches nesting in your sumac," he said as he stepped over the threshold, and I could have hugged him.

So that is what has happened to me now. I have fallen in love with Eric and I am half ashamed and half excited.

I offered Eric a cup of coffee and fussed over him in the most ridiculous way as he drank it. I wondered what interesting outing he had come to propose today and hoped that he was not planning to include Laurel.

He stirred the sugar in his coffee. "I'm afraid I'll have to go to London for a day or two," he said.

My heart sank.

"Pity to go away just when the weather's turned nice — so much to do in the garden," he added.

"Must you really go?" I asked forlornly. What a shame, just when I've suddenly realised how much I need you here, I thought, and I gazed at the floor at a loss for words, amazed at my folly and terrified lest he guess what was in my mind.

"I shall miss you," I said curtly.

"Don't be silly, Prudence," he said. "I'll be back in a day or two and we'll climb into the old jalopy and be on the road again in no time. Where shall we go to? Exmoor? Dartmoor? The Quantocks . . .?" He gave a dry sort of chuckle as if he were laughing at some quite other, private joke, and patted my hand.

I felt confused and silly and altogether at a loss for words. I wondered if his chiropodist friend had anything to do with this sudden plan of departure, but dared not ask.

"It's to do with Morag," he said.

Morag. That was she.

"Her husband's in hospital."

"Her husband!" I couldn't disguise my astonishment. And in my heart there was fear.

"Not a very nice man I'm afraid," Eric went on casually. "He's given her a dreadfully tough time, poor girl."

Morag's husband, it turns out, is an inveterate alcoholic but she, having some kind of lingering affection or perhaps pity for him, has always refused to leave him although he has been making her life a misery for years. Occasionally, when she feels that she can't go on any longer, she escapes for a few days and perhaps comes down to stay with Eric. She is a very, very old friend of Eric's. I hate to think how old and neither can I bear to consider the nature of their intimacy, nor the closeness of their friendship. And now she is taking him away from me.

Suddenly it dawned on me with a wave of blissful relief that, in fact, Morag was probably a friend whom Eric had inherited from his wife. Yes. That must be the case. And she, of course, would be bound to be extra caring of him as the widower of her old friend. But then that explanation didn't really help me. Neither did it, nor does it entirely convince me, as even if Morag was initially Eric's wife's friend there is no doubt about it that she is now his and he has been alone for quite some time.

I suppose that at various times in my life I have longed for some kind of emotional entanglement, yearned for the excitement it might bring, the relief from tedium, the thrill of involvement and above all the feeling of not being passed by, or rather of not allowing life to pass me by. I have wanted to feel what other people felt and I have wanted to know that I, too, was participating in life, not merely watching it go by from the sidelines.

The grass, as Eric would undoubtedly say, is always greener . . . So now, here am I, long past what is normally considered, even in this modern age, to be the proper time for romance, on the other side of the fence at last, yearning for peace of mind, worrying myself sick over an elderly man and eaten up with jealousy for a chiropodist called Morag. Seen from the outside the whole thing would surely appear utterly ridiculous.

Morag's husband has been ill for a while. Cancer of some unmentionable part of the body. According to Eric this has not prevented him from drinking, but rather encouraged him to turn to the bottle to relieve the pain. Poor Morag has been having a terrible time. He's been in and out of hospital which has given her some respite, but she's quite worn out. Last time he was in hospital Eric went to stay with her to hold her hand and cheer her up. That was the time they went to see *The Magic Flute*. It had taken Morag out of herself to go to the opera. But this time Eric didn't think they'd be doing anything like that. Morag's husband was too ill. It could be the end. She'd be round at the hospital most of the time when she wasn't at work.

I am ashamed to say that I have begun to hate Morag. What right has this unknown woman to interrupt the even — or, suddenly, not so even — tenor of my life, with her problems? With her sick husband and her miserable marriage? I imagine that she is a very selfish woman, the sort of person who expects her friends to drop everything for her sake. I wonder what, if anything, she has ever done for Eric.

Dear Eric is so good and kind that he has probably always allowed Morag to trample on him. And now that she is about to be widowed, she will probably eat him alive, take him over, possess him ... even marry him. To be perfectly honest, the thought of poor Eric marrying that woman makes me feel quite ill. I do hope, for his sake, that he will avoid that pitfall. He may well enjoy opera, but I cannot imagine how he could bear to live in London. And as for Morag moving down here! That would be quite out of the question. She could hardly accommodate herself to country life. I know that kind of woman. She would be most unsuited to the country. I do hope that Eric will avoid making so terrible a mistake, the sort of mistake which he might be quite capable of making merely out of pity.

So Eric has gone to London now and I am appalled by the gap his absence leaves in my life and am permanently haunted and tortured by the image of him with that scheming woman. Sometimes I almost wish that Eric had not come into my life so great and so persistent is my anxiety about him and so constantly do I think of him. But then, had he not come into my life, I would have nothing to look forward to now, at this late stage in my time whereas I do have his return to look forward to and further outings in his old jalopy ... provided Morag doesn't keep him for ever. God forbid.

Yesterday Victor and Patricia came to supper, bringing Laurel.

They had not been to see me for some time and I, who usually rather dread their crowding into my little house, was for once glad of their company, as it took my mind off Eric and his absence.

Laurel, I was pleased to see, had a faint fuzz covering her head. She has decided at last to grow her hair again which should at least have been a consolation to Patricia. But Patricia was her usual gloomy self. Laurel, she is sure, has wasted so much time shaving her head and doing other unspeakable things to herself, that she is bound to fail her 'A' levels.

I can hardly see the logic there.

Victor said that he would rather not discuss Laurel any further, as he finds the whole subject of his daughter, her hair, her exams and even her opinions, thoroughly upsetting.

"You're not much of a father," said Laurel, "making remarks like that in front of me. You'll probably give me anorexia if you go on. You could upset me deeply, you know."

"Oh do shut up, Laurel," Patricia said with unaccustomed sharpness.

For once I rather sympathised with Laurel.

Victor had turned his attention to his food and was scrutinising a piece of chicken on the end of his fork in an attempt, I presumed, to blot out any awareness of the presence of his daughter.

"Who would you have liked to have had for a daughter?" Laurel asked her father in a provocative tone. "I would like to have had a father like Eric."

"Mr Janak to you, dear," said Patricia, sharply again.

"Eric," said Laurel, "would be a wonderful father. He's so broad-minded and understanding and, considering how ancient he is, he's really interesting to be with. He can talk about anything."

I was delighted to be talking about Eric.

"I don't think you should spend so much time bothering him," said Patricia. "I'm sure he has better things to do than to think about little girls."

Laurel sniggered.

"Eric is a very kind man," I said. "I'm sure he's delighted to be able to help Laurel in any way he can."

This morning Patricia telephoned to thank me for supper and to discuss Eric's relationship with Laurel,

She was frankly worried. She didn't like what was going on one little bit. Did I think that Eric might perhaps be a little bit funny? You did hear such dreadful things these days – you could never be too careful.

I, too, have had my doubts about Eric's attitude to Laurel, but to Patricia, I would defend him to my eye-teeth. In any case, I told her, I don't know what all the fuss is about as Eric has gone away to London now and goodness only knows when he will get back.

Patricia knew that Eric was in London and that was one of the things that worried her. Laurel had a postcard from him there this morning, and now she is planning to rush off up to London and see him.

Where, I wondered, was my postcard from Eric?

CHAPTER
11

June 10th

My postcard from Eric came this morning. Or rather, my letter. Morag's husband, he tells me, has died. The end came quite peacefully but poor Morag is in a dreadful state. He is planning to stay on in London to help her with the funeral arrangements.

Morag, it appears, has no close relations apart from a sister in Canada. After the funeral she is going to fly out to Vancouver to stay with her sister for a while and "to get away from it all". Everything has been too much for her and she won't be feeling up to going straight back to work immediately after the funeral.

Eric plans to stay with Morag until he has put her safely on her aeroplane by which time he will be glad to get back home. He is missing the country, he says, and is worried that the weeds may be growing too quickly in his garden. He expects to be back in about ten days' time.

I hope that Morag stays with her sister for a very long while. The news that she is to go to Vancouver is the best news I have heard for weeks. The news that she is now a widow I find rather less pleasing.

Oh dear, how I do miss Eric. And to think that there was once a time when his endless calling on me was a source of aggravation. Now I long for his return and find it hard to think about anything else. When I try to read, my mind wanders so that after three or four pages I realise that I have not taken in one single word. The television likewise fails entirely to distract me.

I have decided to try to concentrate on Timothy and on my

memories of that traumatic time in my life when he was so important to me. That may be the one positive way in which I can avoid dwelling on the trauma of the present.

But I must not forget to telephone Patricia to tell her what has happened as it would be no good at all if Laurel took it into her head just now to run up to London in search of Eric. There is something about Patricia which often makes me put off the moment of telephoning her. Perhaps I will speak directly to Laurel.

*   *   *

When Leo came to Blenkinsop's, he came, as he had promised, alone and he came by train. There was no Mrs Hooper and there was no gleaming Porsche. I hoped that they were both things of the past.

I hadn't seen Leo for a while and the first thing I noticed about him was that he had changed. That is to say that he had changed his appearance. His hair was no longer dyed in different shades of mauve, but had returned to its natural blonde colour. At least it had returned to its natural blonde colour enhanced by what I imagined to be some extremely expensive highlights. I wondered at a poor drama student being able to afford such luxury.

Leo appeared on my doorstep, his usual buoyant self.

"Dear Auntie," Leo said in his affected way, "you are a peach to receive me." He was quite aware of all the unanswered letters I had sent him, and no doubt felt that a certain amount of buttering up was required in mitigation for his remiss behaviour.

When I had shown him his bedroom, he suggested that we go to a pub for a drink.

It seemed like a good idea as a change of scenery would no doubt make the evening pass more smoothly, but I did not want to go to any of the local pubs where I knew I would run the risk of finding Blenkinsopians.

Some of my colleagues used to delight in doing the rounds of the local pubs on a Saturday evening in the hope of catching a few red-handed miscreants. I wondered at their having no more agreeable way of spending their evenings and for my own part would have done anything to avoid unnecessary confrontation.

So we drove in my little Renault to a well-known public house some eight or ten miles outside the town.

I do not spend, nor have ever spent, a great deal of time in public houses, but I was pleased to go with Leo to the Black Swan.

He, poor impoverished boy, insisted on buying me a drink and as I sat sipping my gin and tonic, I looked at him sitting opposite me, with his vodka and lime and wondered at the improbability of his parentage. It was quite amazing that Victor and Patricia between them could have produced so handsome a creature. With his newly golden mane, Leo was very good-looking indeed. He waved his hands about in ludicrously camp gestures which did nothing but enhance his natural beauty.

For a moment it even crossed my mind to wonder if perhaps Patricia had been playing fast and loose all those years ago. After all she had taken a long time to conceive her first child. Perhaps Victor was not only enuretic, but sterile. But the idea of Patricia as an adulteress seemed highly unlikely, so, somewhat ashamed at having allowed the thought to cross my mind, albeit not for the first time, I dismissed it.

I asked Leo if he had seen his parents lately, but he had not. He hated to go home because his father never did anything but complain about his chosen profession, producing an endless liturgy of all the pitfalls which lay ahead. His mother, he said, was not much better, always moaning about something.

"Poor Patricia," I said, "she's never had a very cheerful outlook on life."

"But we haven't come here to talk about poor, darling Patricia, have we, dear Auntie," said Leo, running the fingers of his left hand through a golden lock and tossing his head like a young horse.

I noticed around his long neck a thin gold chain from which there hung a heart-shaped locket. Victor would not like that, I thought. Not one little bit. Then as I glanced at the red and blue and turquoise parakeet which adorned Leo's left ear, I remembered the fuss Victor had made when his son had first had it pierced.

Not quite ready and therefore reluctant to embark on the subject which was dear to both our hearts, I returned to the topic of Victor.

"You know," I said, "your father will never be able to reconcile himself to that parrot — nor to that gold chain for that matter."

Leo fingered the heart which hung from the chain.

"It was her last present to me," he said with another toss of his head.

I looked at my drink.

"Marietta's," he said. "We're through, you see. Finished. It's all over. The end of the affair . . ."

"Sh . . ." I said. He seemed to me to be talking dreadfully loudly so that even in the noisy pub people were turning to stare.

Throwing back his magnificent head, he gulped down the last of his drink. I suppose I have always been so fond of Leo partly because he is such an unexpected person to be a member of my family. With his beauty and flamboyant showing-off he is almost as unlikely a nephew for me as a son for Victor.

It was my turn to buy the second round which we would definitely need if we were properly to deal with the matter in hand. I had left a stew to keep warm in the oven for our supper, so we were in no particular hurry.

"Tell me about the summer holidays," I said, venturing at last to come to the point.

"The summer holidays were cataclysmic." He leaned his elbows on the little round pub table as, from behind his folded hands, he gazed at me with an appalling frankness.

There had been the three of them in this villa in Corfu, and right from the beginning Timothy had sulked. So much so that it had become almost impossible to get one word out of him. Marietta was so angry that, much against Leo's better judgment, she decided to leave Timothy alone to sulk while she and Leo went off to drink Retsina and to eat Fetta cheese and houmus in little seaside restaurants.

In fact this arrangement did not please Leo at all because, to be perfectly frank with me, as he said, he only went to Corfu in the first place to be with Timothy.

"I cannot help the way I am," he said. "As a matter of fact I'm perfectly happy that way. Anything's better than being in bed with Marietta Hooper."

"Sh . . ." I said again, both fascinated and appalled at what I was hearing.

"Well, I told you in the first place that I wouldn't succumb. But I had to really. It was dreadful though. Perfectly dreadful! Not my scene you know." He pulled an exaggeratedly disgusted face. "But then she was in love with me. Quite besotted, you see. And I was in love with Timothy. I am in love with him still, the dear boy."

"Oh Leo," I said, "what a muddle. What a dreadful muddle. You shouldn't have done it, you know. You really shouldn't. Your behaviour has not been very laudable, and whatever your *mœurs* you should not use other people." I could not entirely abandon my role as school-mistress and, in any case, there was no doubt about it, he had behaved badly. But what was extraordinary was that he was prepared to be quite so open with me about the whole affair.

In fact Leo has always been open with me ever since he was a little boy when he probably sensed my liking for him. But I certainly never expected to hear such things as this.

"When people are in love," said Leo, "they don't always behave exactly as they should. You must know that, dear Auntie." Then he added, not unkindly but with an air almost of connivance, "Even a spinster lady like you must know that."

I ignored his remark and merely asked him how the rest of the holiday had been.

Apparently he had eventually gone on strike about leaving Timothy alone. For one thing it really was not kind and for another thing Leo couldn't bear to spend all his time with Marietta, being fussed over and petted and spoiled and caressed and praised and kissed.

"She sounds like a pretty silly woman to me," I said tartly, thinking that on the whole she had only got what she deserved.

"She was besotted, I tell you, besotted," he said. "So besotted and so vain that she never realised that what I wanted was Timothy."

"Don't talk like that Leo, please," I said. "Anyway, I think you ought to know that Timothy is now in love with a girl in the school."

Leo had already heard about that from Marietta which was one of the reasons why he had decided to come and see me. He was worried that the girl would do Timothy no good. Timothy was a deeply sensitive, very unhappy boy and a vulnerable one, too. The last thing he needed at this moment was a love affair with an unreliable girl who was probably just playing around with him. She would drop him as soon as she had had enough, which, knowing her kind, would be quite soon. Then what would happen to poor Timothy? He was miserable enough as it was.

At this point I found myself entirely agreeing with everything that Leo said. He only wanted the best for Timothy, as indeed did I. I had to warn him, though, that I did not consider that the best for Timothy included any pressing advances from Leo. That, I insisted, would be quite wrong and I begged him to desist from pestering the boy.

As we drove back to my house, Leo told me that as soon as they had returned from Corfu, he had told Marietta that it was all over between them. She, of course, had been utterly distraught and it was then that she had presented him with the amulet around his neck.

"It's to preserve me from myself," he said with a fey wave of his hand. "But we've remained good friends. Such good friends that I've introduced her to my flatmate. He's ever so good-looking and quite fancies her."

Over supper we discussed endlessly and from every angle what exactly we could do given the status quo and given the fact that, beyond any question of doubt, Timothy's relationship with Natalie must be put to an end before he became too deeply involved.

Leo didn't think that he could speak to Timothy. Sadly he doubted, and rightly, I'm sure, that Timothy would give him the time of day. I certainly did not imagine that I could approach the boy and, as I explained to Leo, I had already rejected the idea of speaking to Natalie.

There remained only one course of action. Leo should speak to Mrs Hooper with whom he was convinced he still had a certain influence and when we heard her reaction we should, as they say, play it by ear.

I cannot now imagine how it was that I then supposed I was acting reasonably nor how I could possibly have thought that by involving Mrs Hooper we were doing anything useful. I knew perfectly well how Timothy felt about his mother and must have been out of my mind to entertain for one instant the idea that he would listen to anything she had to say, particularly concerning affairs of the heart. All I can say is that I was desperately worried for Timothy and in my desperation I was haunted by his pale face and by the terrible look in his sad green eyes as he stood in my kitchen that day asking me if I had ever wished I were dead.

The following morning was a Sunday and while Leo lay slumbering in the spare bedroom I took myself off to church where I prayed hard for Timothy.

Leo didn't surface until nearly one o'clock and then after lunch it was time for him to go back to London.

Almost as soon as Leo had left me I began to feel that the experience of the last twenty-four hours had been a mere dream. If not a dream, it was as though I had been on board ship, somehow removed from the everyday reality of my life to a place where the ordinary rules of behaviour could more easily be flouted. A place where emotion and fantasy took over from common sense.

It seemed strange to think that I had been sitting in the Black Swan with Leo discussing the rather squalid events of his summer holiday in Corfu, events in which I could not help but feel that I was somehow implicated.

I wondered how long it would be before I heard from Leo again, or from Mrs Hooper herself, and decided that until I did I must try to put the whole affair out of my mind as the constant going over and over of it was both upsetting and unconstructive.

But this was more easily said than done. I had taken to sleeping badly, waking regularly at one, or two, or three, and in the haunting loneliness of the small hours my fears for Timothy were only exaggerated. Then, as day broke, I would fall into a deep sleep, only to be woken shortly afterwards by the hurtful shrillness of my alarm clock. As a result of these wretched nights I became tetchy and tearful, a condition which my friends most annoyingly and embarrassingly put down to my age.

As I walked around the school in the daytime, I felt weary and distracted and was all too often confronted by the new Timothy, laughing hand-in-hand with Natalie. He affected not to notice me and never came to see me. Sometimes he skipped his French classes and when he attended them he sat silently in the back of the classroom, barely listening. The work he handed in usually arrived late and was of the poorest possible quality. The time had come for the headmaster to have a word with him.

*   *   *

June 22nd

Eric has come back at last, I am happy to say.

He rang me yesterday evening to say that he was home and horrified by all the weeds in his garden. He has been away for over two weeks. Two long weeks during which time I have managed to get on with some writing and a little gardening, but during which time he has been sorely missed.

Laurel came round to see me one day. Her 'A' levels have started and that morning she had had a paper which she hated. I was surprised at her coming as she and I have never really had much to say to each other. But I was glad to see her in a way, but not because she took my mind off Eric. She certainly didn't do that since she talked about him ceaselessly. So much so that I began to wonder if she doesn't have some kind of a crush on him. But I dismissed the thought as ludicrous. She merely likes to be the centre of attention and he, extraordinarily, is prepared to listen to her nonsense.

She was furious, she told me, with that woman's husband for dying. I could have said that I wasn't too pleased about it myself. She had been planning to go up to London for the day as Eric had promised to take her to the British Museum.

I thought it was just as well that she hadn't been able to go, the week before her exams started being hardly the time to go gadding about the country visiting museums.

Laurel didn't agree. Anyway, she had a new project in mind which she wished to discuss with Eric as soon as he returned.

"What's that?" I asked.

"Never you mind," she said, reverting to her former rude self.

"Well, I hope it's nothing too foolish this time," I said tartly.

As she left I watched her back view disappearing through my garden gate and was suddenly moved by the pathos of the big bottom and the fuzzy head. Poor child, she doesn't have much chance with parents like hers and with a sour spinster school-mistress for an aunt. Perhaps inside that bulky body there is a spark of originality and a free spirit which is striving to escape. I, of all people, should know how she feels.

"Good luck with the rest of your exams," I called faintly after her retreating form.

The day after his return Eric came to supper with me. He refused to come to lunch, saying that he had so many things to catch up with. Letters to write, and he must spend some time in the garden. So I had to wait for him all day. Never has a day seemed longer and when at last I heard the latch click on the garden gate, I felt my heart pounding and my palms sweating.

I opened the door, and there he stood on the step, an old man, weary, white-haired and slightly bent. Just a quite ordinary man who usually speaks in clichés. What on earth is it, I wonder, that makes him so dear to me?

"Eric," I said with unusual warmth and with what I hoped was a touch of softness in my voice, "I am so pleased to see you! So pleased."

To celebrate his return I had bought an especially good bottle of white wine. He certainly looked as though he needed something to cheer him up as his face was drawn and the bags under his eyes seemed to have grown heavier.

I had lit the fire as, despite the time of year, it was a cold evening, and as we sat on either side of the hearth, sipping our wine, I looked at Eric and was happy. Pansy lay at my feet purring like a cat as only Pekineses know how to. But all the while there lurked in the back of my mind a dreadful fear that as soon as Morag returned from Vancouver, Eric would be gone again.

"When she gets back," he said as though to confirm my worst fears, "I shall have to go to London again. She'll be rather lost at first, you know, and I do feel responsible for her in a way."

To myself, I wondered why.

Morag was to stay in Canada for three sweet weeks. I passionately hoped that she would like it there so much that she would stay. Perhaps her sister might even encourage the idea.

"She's a very old friend you see," Eric said, and then, for no apparent reason, "None of us is getting any younger."

Then he told me that Laurel had telephoned him that morning, wanting to come and see him at the week-end.

She had certainly lost no time in finding out that he was back and in pushing herself forward. I wondered at her audacity but, remembering her pathetic dumpy figure leaving my garden the other day, I felt I couldn't be too cross. Besides there was no need to be cross now that I had Eric sitting there opposite me, sipping his wine.

Laurel had a really important plan afoot according to Eric, but he didn't think it sounded particularly sensible. She had been gabbling so excitedly on the telephone that he could hardly make out what she was going on about, but it seems as though, already disillusioned with her newly discovered faith in Hinduism, she has decided to found a new religion of her own.

Just as we had finished our supper and were settling back by the fireside with our coffee there was a tremendous banging on the front door, followed by the harshest and most importunate ringing of the bell.

Who on earth could it have been at that hour, I wondered, as I rose to my feet to go to the door, intensely irritated at the interruption of my cosy tête-à-tête with Eric.

Eric rose too.

"Let me go," he said. "You shouldn't be opening the door at this time of night. You never know who it might be."

It was Laurel. Laurel who had come on her moped and who stood there with, for once it must be admitted, a crash helmet on her head, quite delighted to have tracked down Eric.

I could not allow myself to show my annoyance but neither could I have been more annoyed. The child was becoming a most dreadful nuisance and should not be encouraged to come calling whenever the mood took her.

I tried by various subtle means to convey this message to her without Eric realising that my intentions were anything but friendly. I know how kindly he feels towards Laurel and did not want to upset him.

Laurel, it turned out, had come to the village to look for Eric for whom she had an important document. It was, she explained as she handed him a large brown envelope, the synopsis of her plan.

"But say no more," she added, touching the side of her nose with her forefinger. "Aunt Prudence might not approve."

When she found that Eric was out, she had immediately concluded that there was only one place where he was likely to be and so came straight to my house.

Laurel's behaviour and her manners were frankly intolerable. I decided that sooner or later, preferably sooner, I would have to take her aside and give her a talking to. As it was, my various subtle hints fell on stony ground so that instead of disappearing as soon as she had delivered her missive, she removed her crash helmet, asked for a cup of coffee and sat on the floor in front of the fire, monopolising Eric with her idiotic conversation whilst I sat silently stroking Pansy.

Eventually when Eric said that he was tired and must be

going, he had had a busy day, Laurel too, decided that the time had come for her to be getting home. Her mother, she said, would be out of her mind.

The two of them left together and so ended my longed for evening with Eric.

CHAPTER
12

When Eric and Laurel had gone I set about clearing up the supper, piling the dishes in the sink as I was weary and sad and had not the heart to wash up. All I wanted was to go to bed and nurse my private grief.

Didn't I deserve a little sweetness after a lifetime of stern spinsterhood? But I must not be, and have always tried not to be self-pitying. Besides, for what was I, or am I, to pity myself? I cannot honestly suppose that at our time of life Eric and I are to enter on a whirlwind romance leading to the altar. The very best that I can wish for which would indeed make me happy is that we should continue as we have been up to now, close friends and good companions with perhaps an ever increasing bond of love and affection between us.

Of course I would like Eric to be nearly as fond of me as I am of him. I would like to be needed by him and to have a special place in his heart.

And all these things are still possible despite Laurel and Morag. After all I cannot truly regard an immature and silly teenager as a threat to my happiness even though Eric does appear to have a rather foolish, old man's weakness for her. It is hardly likely that he is actually in love with her.

As for Morag, she presents a threat of an entirely different kind, and a much more real one. But I must try not to dwell too much on the matter. I must try to remain cheerful, friendly and busy.

But I have to admit that as I lay in bed that night I felt my courage fail me. I have been alone for a very long time and as I realised only too well during the weeks of Eric's absence, without his kindly presence I feel very lonely indeed. Without him I would quickly turn into a sad and perhaps rather bitter old lady.

In the morning I felt a little more robust and certainly happier for as I was washing the dishes Eric rang to thank me for supper and to suggest an outing and lunch in a pub. He needed cheering up, he said, and what with Laurel turning up the evening before, he had hardly had time to talk to me properly. My heart soared. Live for the moment, I thought.

"I'm so glad you rang," I said, "I really feel like getting out of the house today. I've been rather down lately. Old age I suppose." There was a lightness in my voice which surely, at that moment, did not reflect my age nor in any way suggest that I was 'down'.

"We're only as young as we feel," said Eric and then rang off.

*   *   *

That term at Blenkinsop's seemed endless. After Leo went back to London I heard nothing from either him or from Mrs Hooper for a while. I was, as they say, eating my heart out, confronted by the permanently disturbing spectacle of Timothy and Natalie wandering around the school in blissful harmony as they both — and more particularly Timothy — trod the path of self-destruction.

Timothy, I knew, had been to see the headmaster who had talked to him at length and kindly about getting down to work and about conforming to school rules which, as we all know, are there for the good of everyone, for the good of the whole school community.

I spoke to the headmaster both before and after he saw Timothy. He told me that he found Timothy a reasonable and polite boy, if a little withdrawn, who had — and I was glad of that — admitted that he had let his work lapse seriously. Timothy had promised the headmaster that he would make a serious attempt to change his ways, saying that he was feeling more positive than he had been formerly.

I wondered if the headmaster had broached the subject of Natalie at all.

He had indeed, he told me. He had reminded Timothy that Natalie was always getting herself into trouble and had put it to him that he, Timothy, might be able to influence her to get down to some work too and to stop fooling around so much. The two of them could, he had suggested, do a great deal to help each other.

I was horrified.

"Help each other!" I cried. "That girl is terrible. She can do him no good at all."

"I think you are rather over-dramatising the whole thing, Prudence," the headmaster said.

I wondered if the headmaster had any conception of the sort of depths of depression to which Timothy had sunk.

"Well, he seems quite cheerful now," he said.

I was furious. Had the man no sensitivity?

"I think the only trouble is to get the boy to see that he must start to work at once if he is to have any chance of passing those exams."

The only trouble indeed. Had Timothy not told me that he was psychologically incapable of concentration at the moment?

In the headmaster's opinion, Timothy was a quiet, rather introverted boy who for obvious reasons concerning his background had found difficulty in making friends and being happy at school. This girl friend seemed to have cheered him up a lot. Given him a bit of confidence and some much needed affection.

Much needed affection! For the past year or more I had been giving Timothy all the affection I possibly could, but apparently to no avail. And now it appeared that a flighty girl was to be the answer to his problems.

I was appalled at the headmaster's lack of common sense and understanding.

Towards the end of that term I was so weary that I had almost given up caring what happened to anyone and was, I felt sure, no longer teaching with my usual efficiency and attention to detail.

This was bad as I hate to let my pupils down. Never until then, in all my teaching career, had I failed to mark work on time nor had I ever been so unenthusiastic in my approach. I needed the rest that the Christmas holidays would surely bring and I needed to sort out my thoughts and my feelings.

My heart still bled for Timothy in his new found bliss which I knew could not last. It hurt me to see him around the school with that hateful girl always showing off at his side, making silly jokes, standing on her head or waving her limbs about in affected attitudes.

Very occasionally Timothy would stop and talk to me in the passage, but he no longer came to tea and as term progressed I had the strange feeling that he had come to resent me. He seemed when he saw me to glower rather than to smile and gradually he ceased talking to me altogether except when obliged to in class. I have to admit that something the headmaster had said to him must have gone home, however, as he now handed work in regularly. Work which was not particularly brilliant, but which was certainly adequate.

So by the last fortnight of term I was in a very overwrought and nervous state and it was at about this time that I heard of Mrs Hooper's imminent arrival. The headmaster told me that she was coming down to see him and that she would like to meet me at the same time. I was surprised by her unwonted concern for her son but thought that perhaps Leo had at last had some influence on her.

As the day of Mrs Hooper's visit approached, I began to grow exceedingly nervous. I could not imagine what she would have to say to me and did not even know whether she was coming as a friend or a foe. It could well be either.

I went over and over in my head what I would say to her along the lines of, 'I'll say such and such' and then she'll say 'so-and-so', then I'll say something else, and so on and so forth until I was utterly sick of all the imaginary conversations echoing through my head.

My pupils must have found me unbearably distracted, and they reacted accordingly. I found that I was allowing them to get away with things that I would never have tolerated before. Elementary mistakes of every kind crept into their work, agreements were forgotten, accents overlooked, irregular verbs unlearned. Shame on you, Prudence.

Next to his office, the headmaster had a sitting room which closely resembled a dentist's waiting room except that it had a drinks cabinet in the corner, but which was generally considered to be a more welcoming place in which to entertain distinguished guests, like visiting lecturers and some especially privileged parents. I was never quite sure exactly what the qualities were which made someone eligible for the sitting-room rather than the office. In Mrs Hooper's case I think it was her amazing prettiness combined with that remarkable confidence in the power to attract which often makes others almost subservient to the very pretty. At least it makes others desperately wish to please them.

At half past twelve on the day of Mrs Hooper's visit, the headmaster summoned me to his sitting-room where he had already been entertaining her for a while alone.

"Ah Prudence," he said, "do come in."

Mrs Hooper was sitting in one of the beige upholstered chairs, her delicate legs crossed, her head tilted prettily to one side with what looked like a gin and tonic in one hand.

"Mrs Hooper," said the headmaster, "this is Miss Fishbourne."

Mrs Hooper did not rise from her chair but put down her drink, uncrossed her legs and leaned forward, her head still on one side, one bangled arm outstretched to offer me her hand.

I shook it perhaps rather awkwardly. She looked directly at me. Her eyes were large, and green like her son's.

"I'm very pleased to meet you — at last," she said in a pretty piping tone. And added, with a question in her voice, "I think I know your nephew, Leo?"

I thought she did too.

"Now Prudence, let me get you a glass of sherry," said the headmaster rubbing his hands together and leaning forward in a caring way, slightly gauchely I thought.

"Sweet or dry?" he enquired from beside the drinks cabinet.

"Dry," I replied in a tone that must surely have been drier than the driest fino.

The headmaster handed me my drink and after a few desultory remarks about the approach of Christmas which seemed to come round more quickly every year, and the bitterness of the weather, he suggested that we might excuse him as he had a few things which needed his urgent attention and that we might like to have a chat.

He shook Mrs Hooper's hand with unusual warmth, looking at her in just that way that I have, throughout my life, observed men looking at pretty women, half confident, half pleading for a special – however tiny – place in their hearts.

I, as is always the case at such moments, became acutely aware of my large nose, large feet, large frame.

When the headmaster had at last disappeared, I sat down gratefully in an armchair, took a sip of my sherry and wondered where we would go from there.

Mrs Hooper did not seem to be in the least bit antagonistic to me. Not that she had any reason to be, of course.

She thanked me for having been kind to Timothy in the past and told me how desperately worried she had been about the boy.

"Desperately!" she added in the tones of a bad actress who has no understanding of the concept of desperation.

"He has always begged me to take him away from the school," she said. "But things have been difficult at home." She waved her hand airily. "My husband and I are separated – our marriage didn't work out." She opened her green eyes in pained innocence.

"I'm very sorry," I said, wondering where the conversation was leading.

She leaned forward earnestly and tapped her chest with a long rosy-red fingernail. "I," she said, "am a very sensitive person. Timothy's father, on the other hand, is not at all sensitive. He could never understand my needs – in fact, I am afraid to say, he is an extremely selfish man. I, of course, would have loved nothing more than to keep Timothy at home with me. I am a particularly maternal woman you see, Miss Fishbourne. But my husband made life quite impossible for us at home and so there was no alternative but to send him away to school – well, he would have had to go anyway even if we hadn't lived in Saudi Arabia. I was heartbroken when Timothy went away for the first time – I didn't know how I was going to manage without him . . ."

And so she went on and on and on.

Eventually she came to the point.

"I have been talking to Leo," she said and for a moment had the good grace to glance at the ground. "He's such a kind boy," she went on, "and really worried about Timothy. He has persuaded me that the time has come for Timothy to leave school. That is to say he feels that Timothy is too old to continue boarding and besides it has made the poor darling so unhappy in the past. No. He shall come back to London and live with me and go to day school. Leo will be around to keep an eye on him . . ."

I gasped.

Leo would be around to keep an eye on him. Treacherous Leo.

And what would I do . . ? What indeed? I felt the bottom falling out of my world. My head spun.

Somehow I managed to pull myself together enough to plead with Mrs Hooper to change her mind.

To take Timothy away from school at this juncture would be fatal for his exams. He was beginning to work a little harder, to produce results, to be a little happier, he was settling in at last, and so forth.

But Mrs Hooper was adamant.

She was touched by my concern for Timothy but her mind was made up. She had told the headmaster of her decision and as soon as she returned to London she would confirm that decision in writing. Timothy would not be returning to Blenkinsop's in January.

"If you take him away so suddenly," I tried one desperate last attempt to sway her, "you may have to forfeit next term's fees."

"Geoffrey," she said, rising to her feet, "can take care of that. He's got plenty of money." She laughed a silly, tinkling laugh and put out her hand.

"Well," she said, "I must be off now and find my little boy. I'm taking him out to lunch. So nice to have met you Miss Fishbourne." She laughed her silly, tinkling laugh again and was gone.

Although I suppose that good manners should really have prompted me to accompany her, I allowed her a moment or two to get away before leaving the sitting-room myself.

The first person I met as I made my way down the passage was one of the Spanish teachers with whom I was friendly.

"Good Lord, Prudence!" she exclaimed. "What on earth is the matter with you? You look as if you've seen a ghost. Are you feeling all right?"

I felt as if I had seen a ghost, too.

"You need a break," she went on. "Perhaps you need someone to talk to." She looked at her watch. "Come home with me," she said, "there'll be no one there. We can have a bite of lunch and a chat."

Her husband, who was a civil engineer and whom I didn't like very much, was away, but even so and although I was touched by her kindness, I didn't feel very much like accepting her invitation. I wanted to be alone, and I wanted the security and comfort of my own house.

*　　　*　　　*

Eric has been home for about ten days now and Laurel who has finished her exams has gone to London with a girl-friend to celebrate and to attend some, no doubt dreadful, pop concert.

Leo telephoned on Thursday to say that he is staying with his parents for a few days and would I come over for lunch.

So yesterday I went to lunch with Victor and Patricia. They are about to go on holiday but are in a shared fever of anguish about what Laurel will get up to while they are away. She refuses to accompany them to the Lake District and has renounced her own plans to go hitch-hiking on the Continent. She intends to

136

spend the summer at home disseminating her new religion throughout the West Country and awaiting her exam results. She doesn't know what she is going to do after that.

Meanwhile Victor is persuaded that she will forget to feed the goldfish and that he will return from the North to find it floating, belly-up in a bowl of fetid water. He does not want to come home to that.

Patricia begs me to keep an eye on Laurel. I am the only person with any control over Laurel. The only one she will listen to.

I am not so sure about that.

Patricia doesn't count Eric because, with all due respect to me and to my own friendship with Eric, Patricia does not at all approve of his association with her daughter.

I wish we didn't have to talk about Eric and Laurel like that. It makes me feel uncomfortable.

After lunch Leo suggests that he and I and Pansy go for a walk. I am glad to get out of the house.

There is a pretty walk which takes us up the lane, through a wood, across a field and back through the churchyard. The sun is breaking through the clouds and it is a warm day.

Leo is in tremendously good form despite his father's attempts to cast him into a Stygian gloom.

"I've got this part in a film," he says as we walk. "It's a great part but I cannot discuss it in front of my parents. The very thought of it upsets Father even more than the prospect of finding a dead goldfish when he comes back from his ludicrous holiday."

Leo is walking with a spring in his step.

"What is it?" I ask eagerly, so happy to think that success may be coming his way at last.

It is absolutely wonderful this film. A contemporary adaptation of *La Dame aux Camélias* in which the consumptive Marguerite Gautier is replaced by an AIDS-stricken boy called Martin and played by Leo. The part of Armand Duval is to be taken by a great star. Leo names a really famous actor.

Filming starts next month on location in Romney Marsh

where Martin and Armand are living out their country idyll. Leo is very, very excited. It is hardly surprising that he can talk of little else for most of the duration of our walk. After all I cannot remember when Leo was last in work and nothing he has ever done yet has been remotely important. He has had the occasional walk-on part in a television play, but nothing more.

I rejoice for Leo and, somewhat maliciously, laugh to myself at the prospect of Victor's discomfort. He, I know, will find it very difficult to hold up his head in his office when it becomes known that his son is playing a homosexual hero in a feature film.

"Do you think your father will ever see the film?" I ask Leo.

"Good Lord, no!" Leo exclaims. "He will never dare."

"Poor Victor," I say, "he should be delighted by your success."

"Mother's no better," says Leo. "She is so upset because she thinks I'm for ever and ever doomed to be type-cast as a beautiful young man." He twists his body dramatically and flings back his head. "Which is of course exactly what I am. An amazingly beautiful young man." He laughs almost hysterically.

Suddenly he becomes serious and quite changes the tone of the conversation.

Then we were walking through a wide green field where a herd of lazy brown and white cows stretched out their long necks and swayed their heads from side to side as they gazed at us with mild curiosity. Pansy trotted along at my heels, too old and too wise now to care about cows.

"I think someone ought to speak to Laurel," Leo said, "before she does anything too, too drastically silly."

I wonder what he means.

"She is," he says, "potty, quite potty about that old man of yours."

"What old man of mine?" I replied foolishly and indignantly.

"Your Eric," he said.

"Hardly *my* Eric," I replied tartly.

"Oh come along dear Auntie . . ." Leo said, "*plus ça change . . .*," and he jumped, elfin-like, over a small branch blown down from some tree, which lay in his path.

"Last time it was you and me and Timothy," he said. "You and me and Timothy, and I suppose Marietta; and now it's you and Laurel and Eric. *Plus ça change ... plus ça change...*," he chanted.

"Come along Pansy," I said sharply, turning to look at my dog. "I don't know what you mean," I said rather savagely, "about you and me and Timothy. Nor do I see what Timothy and Laurel and Eric can possibly have to do with one another."

"Ah, but I can," Leo sighed languidly. "And of course, if you are honest with yourself, you too will see what I mean."

I honest with myself? I have always prided myself on being honest with myself. I have, as I have already explained, done my best throughout my life to be honest with myself, to examine my motives and to understand my actions.

At a remarkably early age I recognised the role which I was destined to play in life. It is not an exciting one but I have done all I can to adapt to it, to face up to it and to be content with it and yet there I was, only yesterday afternoon, being confronted by my nephew with the suggestion that I delude myself.

"Now come on, Leo," I said, half humorously, half sharply, "I am not the kind of person who goes around fooling herself. I hardly think you can accuse me of that."

"Don't be offended," said Leo, taking hold of my hand and giving it a friendly squeeze. "But do avow that you were a tinsy-winsy-winsy bit in love with Timothy." Then he added, "I certainly was and, what is more, I owned up at the time."

I didn't know where to look and yet as he spoke I admitted to myself for perhaps the very first time that although I could not have been really, truly in love with Timothy since he was only a child then and I was an adult woman, well into middle age, I had perhaps been bordering on that condition. Suddenly I was quite indignant. I had not felt about Timothy the way I now feel about Eric. Surely not.

And then I was overcome with embarrassment. What on earth was I doing having such a conversation as this with Leo? What was my private life to do with him? And why was he still holding my hand?

I disentangled my hand and quickened my pace. We were

139

about to enter the churchyard and would soon be back at the house.

"You shouldn't be so embarrassed," said Leo, turning and walking backwards so that he could look straight at me.

"If you walk backwards like that, you'll fall over and hurt yourself," I said as though I were talking to a child.

"Well, let's forget Timothy for the moment," said Leo, still walking backwards. "Let's forget his beautiful green eyes and his golden hair and his whole sweet self and let's think about Eric instead." He laughed. "He's quite good-looking you know." Then he added cruelly, "and your age-group too, for a change."

As soon as he had spoken he regretted what he had said, rushed to my side and put both arms round me.

"Darling Auntie," he said, "that was beastly. I'm so, so sorry." And he planted an awkward wet kiss on my cheek.

I pushed him away crossly.

"Come on Leo," I said, "stop being so silly and let's get on with our walk."

But he insisted. He had to talk about Eric and Laurel. He knew that I loved Eric. Of course I did not admit as much but I wondered how on earth he had guessed.

"It's perfectly obvious that you love Eric," he said. "It's obvious from the way you talk about him and from the way you behave when he's around."

I did not demean myself to enquire exactly how I behave when Eric is around which in any way differs from how I behave when he is not around.

"It is also perfectly obvious that Laurel is equally in love with Eric. She is quite, quite besotted about him."

I cannot say that I cared for the comparison between myself and Laurel.

"What on earth Eric feels about Laurel, I have no idea," said Leo.

We were walking through the churchyard by then.

"Perhaps he loves her too," he went on. "Stranger things have happened. Stranger things indeed." He slipped his hand through my arm and said, "Please don't be cross with me. You see I am on your side this time. Really on your side. Laurel is a reckless girl. She would do anything. Anything. I just wanted to warn you that's all, because you see I'm fond of you and I would like you to be happy."

We walked on for a moment in silence until we came out at the other side of the churchyard into the village street.

Then Leo said, "You know neither of us behaved particularly well last time."

"I don't know why you should say that," I snapped. But I did really, and for the first time I felt a little ashamed and also suddenly amazed by Leo's honesty with himself. From start to finish, throughout the whole Timothy episode, he had never denied his motives, however vile. And at times they had certainly been vile.

"Anyway, this time it's all different," he said. "This time you're going to be happy and I'll see to it. Last time we were responsible for what happened. Entirely responsible. Both of us. Well, let's just be responsible again. After all, this time it's in a better cause." He turned to look at me. "You have to admit that."

I would admit nothing.

"Well, if you refuse to talk to Laurel, I shall have to take the child in hand, though I sometimes doubt that she has a proper respect for her brother," he said.

By the time we reached the house, Leo was talking about prisoners of conscience.

How he got on to them, I have no idea. In any case I was barely listening to what he was saying. I was thinking about Eric. And missing him. Laurel, I thought, was not really a problem.

Leo doesn't know about Morag.

CHAPTER
13

On Saturday night I lay awake for hours going over and over in my mind what Leo had said.

I was and am still quite appalled by his suggestion that I was 'in love' with Timothy, a suggestion which I regard as totally absurd although I do admit, and always have done, that I was exceptionally fond of him. A little fonder even than I should have been. But 'in love'? No. That cannot be right.

For the past few months I have been writing this memoir as much as anything in order to sort out my emotions about Timothy and somehow to put the whole episode into perspective. As I say, I have never denied my fondness for Timothy, a fondness which probably prevented me from seeing things in proportion at the time.

Afterwards I tried to put the whole matter out of my mind although I know that it was and always has been there, never far from the surface of my consciousness. To think about it was to induce sleepless nights, embarrassment, hurt, humiliation. But in the quiet of my retirement cottage, I decided that the time had come to put the record straight. Did I behave as I should have done at the time? If not, where did I go wrong? I sometimes feel slightly uncomfortable at the memory of my responsibility for the part played by Leo, but I did then think that I was only acting for Timothy's good. Perhaps, indeed, I have nothing to reproach myself with.

Be that as it may, the writing has clearly been cathartic as, until Saturday when Leo started talking to me about being 'in love', I have been feeling so much better about the whole incident, almost as though it didn't really matter to me any more.

Until Leo turned up with his rude reminders of the past, it was as though it only ever existed in my imagination. It had at least, or so I thought, lost its power to hurt.

Perhaps my new life, the move away from the school with all its associations and my friendship with Eric have all played a part in truly relegating my anxieties about Timothy to the past.

And yet, that night as I lay in bed, thinking of my walk with Leo, the whole thing once again began to assume gigantic proportions in my mind so that for the time being, I even forgot to worry about Eric and Morag.

Of course Morag is still safely in Canada at the moment. Long may she remain there.

*　　　*　　　*

The very next day after Mrs Hooper came to Blenkinsop's I was taking Pansy for a run around an icy rugby pitch when I met Timothy and Natalie. It was a Sunday morning and Pansy, who was a good deal younger then and who has always liked the cold weather, was bounding along ahead of me.

As I walked, my thoughts were entirely concerned with Timothy. I could not imagine how he would possibly pass any exams at all if he left school in the middle of the 'O' level year. His mother was behaving in a very irresponsible fashion, and, as for his father, he apparently showed no interest whatsoever in his son's education.

Timothy, I knew, would hate to live with his mother all the time and I wondered how he would react to her sudden decision to remove him from the school.

I wondered too in what way I would be able to help him and how I could manage to get up to London often enough to keep an eye on him. As for Leo keeping an eye on him – well, that hardly seemed suitable to me.

So I was thinking along these lines when suddenly there was

Timothy walking towards me across the frozen grass with Natalie at his side.

My heart missed a beat and I felt myself grow very tense. They must have seen me, and within a moment or two we would come face to face with each other and someone would have to say something.

Timothy stopped in front of me and stood there looking at me solemnly from under a red-gold lock of hair. Natalie stood two steps behind him. She had bright red gloves on and the tips of her fingers only were stuck into her blazer pockets. She wore an extraordinarily tight skirt and had wound round her neck a long, long scarf striped with every colour of the rainbow. She just stood there with one knee bent and stared at me coldly.

There was a slight pause before I said, brightly,

"Hello you two," and then added fatuously. "Out for a nice walk then?"

Natalie said nothing.

Timothy seemed to put his shoulders back and raise his chin.

"You have been talking to my mother," he said in an angry voice. "You had no business to talk to my mother . . ."

"Timothy!" I tried to interrupt him to say that it was his mother who had asked to see me, not the other way round, but he went on speaking.

"You and Leo," he said, "between you, you have done nothing but interfere. And between you you have tried to wreck my life, and all because you are both jealous of my friendship with Natalie."

I was appalled at what I heard and opened my mouth to interrupt again, but no words came out and Natalie still stood there staring.

"And now," he went on, "just when I'm happy, my mother plans to take me away from here and away from Natalie. She wants me to live with her as a live bait for Leo. And it's all your fault."

I could not believe that Timothy was talking to me like that. Surely he must have known that I, who had cared so much for him, would never act without having his best interests at heart.

The idea that I had connived with Leo was quite preposterous. I wanted to put out my hand and touch him, to wipe the anger from his face.

"Timothy," I said, "I love you, how could I want to 'wreck your life'?"

Natalie's lip curled in a sneer.

"I used to think you were quite decent," said Timothy, reverting to a childish idiom. "But I was wrong. And my mother needn't think I'm going to do what she wants because I'm not." He half turned towards Natalie, jerked his head in an uncharacteristically arrogant fashion, and said,

"Come on Natalie, we're going." And they both turned and walked away without another word, leaving me there on the frosty grass with my mouth hanging open.

All I could think as they strode away, was how magnificent Timothy looked when angry, with his shoulders back and his green eyes flashing.

When they had gone I began to worry about the incident and decided that before the end of term I must see Timothy alone. He and I had some talking to do.

The following day, which must have been a Monday and only a week or ten days before the end of term, I was suddenly called out of class in the middle of the morning to see the headmaster. I could not imagine what on earth he could want me for so urgently.

This time he was not in his sitting-room, but in his office and he had abandoned his suave social manner for a more formidable, dominating one.

"Come in and sit down, Prudence," he said curtly, as I entered the office.

I sat down in the chair he indicated which faced his desk and he sat at the desk, leaned back in his swivel chair, crossed his legs, folded his arms, put his head back and stared at me hard and in silence for a moment or two. This, I supposed, was the treatment which he gave to recalcitrant teenagers. I felt somewhat indignant. I was no recalcitrant teenager, but a respected member of staff.

"So what," he eventually enquired, "precisely what do you know about the whereabouts of Timothy Hooper and Natalie Knight?"

I was completely taken by surprise.

What, I wondered, should I know about their whereabouts? As far as I was concerned they were probably attending some class or other. Or perhaps the approach of the Christmas holidays had made them think that they could begin to slack off. If so they were making a great mistake and would surely find themselves in trouble.

"So you haven't heard," said the headmaster, leaning forward now with his left fore-arm on the desk, and with his right hand holding the corner of his spectacles as he glared over them stilly at me.

"Heard what?" I asked.

"I am amazed that you should be the last to hear," he said settling back in his chair again. "I had imagined that you might have been able to help." He looked very angry.

"I have no idea what you are talking about," I said, getting angry myself. Neither had I any idea why he continued to treat me as a recalcitrant pupil.

"Well then, I had better tell you," he said, removing his spectacles and twirling them around in the air with affected nonchalance.

He was beginning to annoy me.

"If you go on doing that you'll break those spectacles," I wanted to say. But I held my tongue.

"Timothy and Natalie have run away," the headmaster announced. "They were discovered this morning to be missing, but on further investigation it transpires that they were seen boarding a train yesterday afternoon. We have of course contacted both Mrs Hooper and Mrs Knight. They have heard nothing and are quite understandably deeply distressed."

The headmaster paused and then, with his middle finger and his thumb, he slowly and carefully moved a stone paperweight which lay on his desk, a fraction of an inch.

"You, Prudence," he said, "were seen talking to Timothy

146

Hooper and Natalie Knight on the rugby pitch at 10.30 a.m. yesterday morning. What was the subject of your conversation?"

I was amazed at the headmaster's impudence.

"They were not so foolish as to tell me that they were planning to run away," I said.

"I asked you," he said, moving the paperweight another quarter of an inch, "what was the subject of your conversation."

I could have lost my temper, but decided instead to say, "Timothy told me that he was beginning to be happy at school and that he did not want to leave. I assumed that he intended to persuade his mother to allow him to stay here."

The headmaster had to believe me, and in effect, what I had told him was the truth.

Nothing more was heard about the whereabouts of Timothy and Natalie that term. Rumours flew around the school proclaiming that they had gone to Gretna Green or America or Bali, but in fact no one ever discovered where they were.

The headmaster was very, very angry indeed particularly when a tabloid newspaper printed a double page spread on 'how top people learn about sex at exclusive (£2000 a term) public school'. No doubt he was initially charmed and lulled into a false sense of security by the bright young girl who had been asked to do a piece for the woman's page of her newspaper.

As a result of all the drama and of the uncertainty which surrounded Timothy's and Natalie's disappearance, an atmosphere of impending doom hung over the school for what remained of that term.

The police came and almost everyone who had spoken to Natalie or Timothy during the last weeks was questioned. No one knew anything. Only Natalie's mother had received a card from her daughter, posted at the station on the Sunday she left. Apparently it merely said something along the lines of 'Don't worry, we are all right and will be in touch soon.' That was all. They both had a little bit of money which they had taken out of their banks, so they might have gone almost anywhere.

Leo telephoned me, distraught, but I had nothing to tell him, nor did he have anything to tell me.

Eventually the term ground to a close and we all dispersed for Christmas with an immense feeling of relief.

Which is not to say that I didn't continue to worry myself sick about what had become of Timothy. I dreamed of him at night and, by day, could forever see him in my mind's eye as I had seen him on that last Sunday morning, striding angrily away from me across the frozen rugby field.

It was some time before I discovered what eventually became of him.

And still to this day the vision of him striding across that rugby field with Natalie at his side is as vivid to me as it was then.

*   *   *

Eric and I have been having a lovely time for the past two weeks. We have seen each other nearly every day and have enjoyed a variety of outings. Picnics, walks, concerts. We even went to the cinema one evening.

Despite his gloomy prognoses, his garden is overflowing with vegetables and I have bought a cookery book full of wonderful ideas for serving peas and beans and fresh young spinach.

We have been very happy and are strangely relaxed in each other's company. I have even come to treasure the inevitable soothing clichés, and no longer mind how slowly he eats.

The weather has been fine and we have sat on the beach or in each other's gardens admiring the birds, the butterflies and the flowers. It has been a very peaceful time interrupted only occasionally by Laurel barging in with pamphlets about her new religion in which God walks the earth masquerading as an okapi or some such nonsense.

Why an okapi? I haven't bothered to ask her as I have no time for such gibberish. But Eric is so kind that he listens to her patiently and gently advises her that her religion is not really likely to take a hold despite the fact that she spends all day pushing advertisements for it under the wipers of the cars in all the town car parks.

I am surprised at Eric's patience with Laurel who has been told by Leo to stop making such a nuisance of herself. Sometimes I do still wonder if he hasn't a slightly indelicate weakness for her. But that seems impossible so I try to put the idea out of my mind and I like to think instead that perhaps Eric is kind to Laurel out of deference to me. After all I am beginning to think that Eric must be quite fond of me. If he isn't, he would surely not want to spend so many hours in my company.

Only the other day he said to me, "Prudence, I don't know what's come over you lately. You look so well. Ten years younger I should say." Happiness works wonders for one's looks, but I have to admit to taking a little extra care with my appearance these days. I wanted to take his hand and say, "Don't you realise, Eric, it's because of you." But instead I just smiled.

During all this time we have not mentioned Morag once.

July 29th

It must be days now since I wrote those fatal last words and I have not had the heart to return to this diary since. Not since the day when Eric appeared at my door looking drawn and old and distraught with, I couldn't help noticing, his fly-buttons undone.

"What on earth is the matter?" I asked him.

"It's Morag," he said. "Poor Morag. She's back in London and seems quite unable to cope alone. Funny really, when you think what a frightful fellow that husband of hers was."

We went into the kitchen and he sat down. I offered him a cup of coffee. He really looked as if he could do with a tot of brandy or some medicinal whisky, but it was only nine o'clock in the morning.

He put his elbows on the kitchen table and his head in his hands.

"I had her on the telephone for hours last night. She said it was all right while she was in Canada. But ever since she's been back, she's been all over the place.' He looked up at me.

"She's a very old friend you know, Prudence," he said. "A

149

very old friend indeed. And now she's alone in the world, I feel I ought to go to her."

I turned away with a lump in my throat.

So that, I thought dramatically, is the end of my little idyll. Ah well.

"I don't know how long I'll be away," he said, "but I really must go and look after her."

"And what about me?" I wanted to scream. But years of well-trained spinsterhood forbade me to speak out of turn.

"She's talking about retiring early," he said. "It seems she can't face work any more. I may bring her back down here with me. God alone knows!" He sipped his coffee. "Well, it's an ill wind . . ." he said.

Bring her back down here, I thought. And I would have to smile and go to the wedding and be their friend. I hated Morag.

"Have you had breakfast?" I asked Eric gently.

No, he hadn't. He'd been in too much of a rush.

I boiled him an egg and made him some toast and put a jar of home-made marmalade on the table and made some fresh coffee and told him I'd miss him.

When he said good-bye, he squeezed my hand and kissed my cheek and said, "You're a wonderful person and a good friend. Thank you for everything."

I could not prevent two large tears from rolling down my cheeks. I cannot imagine what he must have thought of me.

That afternoon Eric took the train to London. Laurel went with him. She had apparently to distribute her fatuous leaflets at London zoo. I thought it was high time Victor and Patricia came home and shook that girl.

Since Eric has been gone I have enjoyed nothing. How foolish I was at so late a stage in my life to allow my guard to slip and to let myself develop so strong a feeling for another human being. I should have been content with my dog, and with the role which I so sensibly assumed all those years ago. I was not cut out for love then, and at my age it is nothing short of ridiculous. And very painful.

Eric has written to me of course. But that is not the same as his being here. Besides he writes of nothing but Morag and how I hate to think of him cosily settled into her flat.

Laurel is forever going backwards and forwards to London with her silly pamphlets. I cannot imagine how she can afford the train fares. She tells me, rather disconsolately, that her religion is not having the immediate impact which she had hoped it would. But she is not prepared to give up yet.

Meanwhile she spends a great deal of time with Eric and Morag when she goes on these trips to London. She says that she has even come to like Morag who is very kind to her and allows her to stay in the flat whenever she wants. That leaves me out in the cold.

But I must try not to be sorry for myself.

That was not easy this morning when Eric's most recent letter arrived.

He has decided to stay in London with Morag. He will miss the country dreadfully, and his garden. He will miss me too and all our enjoyable outings but he hopes that very soon I will come and stay and meet Morag. Somehow he feels that things were meant to turn out this way.

I honestly felt so weary when I read that letter that I had no further desire to go on living. It would have been quite all right by me if just then, sitting as I was at my kitchen table, I had quietly and peacefully passed away.

I suppose I must have sat for hours at that table, too weary to move, too weary even to cry.

Then as the morning wore on I began to grow angry. I was angry with Morag for winning, angry with myself for letting Eric go so meekly and angry with Eric for being so wet. I cannot believe that he is doing what he really wants.

This afternoon I summoned up enough strength to go out, and even to walk towards Eric's house. Since he left I have not liked to walk past his cottage but have tended to take Pansy in the other direction, as the sight of it standing there empty and the memories of all the happy times I have spent there are too painful. Besides it hurts my feelings to see the weeds encroaching on the flowerbeds and the vegetables wasting away, unharvested.

I put Pansy on her lead and told her that we were going for a little walk. She wagged her old tail and looked quite happy, oblivious of the sorrow in her mistress's heart.

We walked down the road briskly. The sky was grey and it looked like rain.

Eric's house is only a three minute walk away from mine which is the last – or first – house in the village. It is round the bend in the lane on the opposite side of the road.

As we approached the bend I heard a peculiar banging. For some strange reason it reminded me of the hacking sound at the end of *The Cherry Orchard* when all the trees are being cut down.

It didn't really occur to me to wonder what the noise was, but as we rounded the corner I was confronted by the full horror of my present and future interminable loneliness.

There, at Eric's garden gate, were two young men in suits nailing a board to a post. The board flaunted the name of our local estate agent and on it was written in large red letters, "For Sale".

CHAPTER
14

The days are drawing in and the summer is well and truly over. Eric seems to have been gone for an age now. I suppose in fact it must be nearly three months since he went to live in London with Morag.

I am trying to come to terms with my loneliness, but it is not easy. Perhaps I never realised quite to what extent I depended on Eric's company and neighbourliness. My little garden is looking untidy and needs to be put to bed for the winter, yet somehow I have no heart for the task. Had Eric been here, he would have helped me with the heavier jobs and would most certainly have admired the end result. I wish he could see the mass of cyclamen under the apple tree, the Japanese anemones and the hips on the rugosa rose. They are all so beautiful in their sad autumnal way.

It seems strange to me that some people claim to love the autumn best of all the seasons. I have always found it saddens me to watch the dying year, to see the leaves fall and the flowers fade. This autumn is certainly as sad as any I can remember. I only hope that the winter will be a short one and that when the spring comes round again I shall be able to regain at least some enthusiasm for my garden.

The melancholy I feel was hardly alleviated two days ago when I was in the village shop. Just as I was putting my few small purchases in my basket a woman came in and announced eagerly that Mr Janak's house has been sold at last. Had we heard?

I looked at the ground. The shopkeeper looked at me.

"Miss Fishbourne would know about that, wouldn't you?" she asked.

I said that I knew nothing.

"I expect you'll be glad when there's someone living in that house," she went on brightly. "It must be lonely stuck out there on the end of the village like that, without even a neighbour since Mr Janak left."

"Not really," I lied.

The shopkeeper folded her arms and wriggled her shoulders.

"Brrr," she said, "aren't you frightened night-times? I would be. You get some funny people around these days you know."

If I were frightened, such remarks, I thought, would hardly be helpful.

The woman who had brought the news about Eric's house was keen to tell us more.

"It seems he's a retired admiral. The man who's bought Mr Janak's house I mean. My neighbour's seen him, says he's ever so nice looking. He must have plenty of money, too . . ." She named a ridiculous sum. "That's what they say he paid for the house."

"What's his wife like?" the shopkeeper asked.

"I think he's a widower," the other woman replied.

"Another single gentleman," said the shopkeeper. "That'll be nice for you, Miss Fishbourne." She nodded at me and laughed a silly, friendly laugh.

On the way home as Pansy and I walked past Eric's house a car drew up and a tall, nice looking man with thick white hair and a straight back got out.

That, I thought sadly, must be the admiral. My new neighbour. I was in no mood for new neighbours. I sighed quietly to myself and passed on.

*　　　*　　　*

The rumours concerning Timothy and Natalie did not die down for a long time and it was nearly five years before I finally discovered what had happened to them. In fact it was only last year, just before I retired, that I eventually heard.

During those final four years in which I worked at Blenkinsop's I began to feel that I was losing my touch as a teacher. I do not know whether this was in any way due to the trauma of the Timothy episode, or if I was merely growing too old and too tired to throw myself wholeheartedly into the job. However that may have been, I found my life-long enthusiasm for teaching was waning, and I also found it increasingly difficult to communicate with young people. I am afraid that this attitude of mine was to some extent reflected in my pupils' examinations. Up until that time the French results at 'O' and 'A' level had always been among the best in the school.

I tried to explain away the disappointing grades by persuading myself that the children were not as bright as they had been in past years, but I cannot honestly claim this to have been absolutely true.

There were times during those years when I felt that life had very little left to offer me. What indeed did I ever look forward to? The occasional trip to France for a week or two with a colleague, Pansy welcoming me home after her two weeks in the kennels, and then, of course, retirement. But what, I wondered, had retirement to offer?

In darker moments it seemed as if, from then onwards, it would be downhill all the way.

But I am not naturally of a despairing disposition, so that I did in fact rally and began to look forward to my retirement with increasing delight. I looked forward to moving back to the West Country, to finding a new house and a new way of life.

Perhaps it was not entirely surprising if, after so many years in the same establishment, I began to weary of the monotonous repetition of the school year. But there it was. I had chosen that way of life and for the most part I enjoyed it and found myself well suited to it.

Of course, for all my failing enthusiasm, those last years were not entirely bad. Just a little flat, I think, so that when the time eventually came for me to shake the dust of Blenkinsop's from my feet, I was, despite the well-worn French saying, *partir c'est mourir un peu*, more glad than sad.

My old friends I could keep in touch with and a new life lay ahead.

Although the rumours about Timothy and Natalie did eventually die down, I never ever lost that nagging feeling of fear which struck me so hard when I first heard of their disappearance.

I used to dream about Timothy almost every night. Dreadful anxiety dreams in which I was always somehow to blame for some appalling disaster.

Whether or not the headmaster ever knew what became of those two, I shall never know, but I was certainly too proud to ask him and assumed that had he in fact known, he must have had the decency to tell me. I had the feeling that the other members of staff rather avoided the subject of Timothy and Natalie in my presence.

Leo might perhaps have been able to help if, shortly after Timothy ran away, he had not been supplanted in Mrs Hooper's affections by her hairdresser. Until then, quite dissatisfied with his handsome flat-mate, she had been persistently manipulating to get Leo back. All this would in the normal course of events have pleased me, but now it meant that Leo was no longer in touch with Mrs Hooper and so could not find out from her what had happened to Timothy.

Marietta, Leo told me, was a real bitch where her old lovers were concerned. She didn't believe in keeping them as friends. Oh no. Not she. He even felt quite sorry for the hairdresser who surely had no idea of the vituperation that lay in wait for him when the end came as it inevitably would.

Leo had been called every name under the sun. He was surprised at the breadth of Marietta's vocabulary. Not that it was the sort of vocabulary one would have expected to hear from a lady.

Marietta had accused Leo of seducing her in order to get at her son and she had blamed him entirely for Timothy and Natalie having run away.

I was not so much surprised to learn about the breadth of her vocabulary, as amazed that she had at last tumbled to the reality of Leo's intentions. She had not struck me as a very perceptive person, to say the least.

So Leo and I were left in the dark about Timothy, both suffering quietly in our separate ways, and both, after the initial shock, reluctant to discuss the subject with each other. Leo, I suspect, being young and resilient, was able to put the matter out of his mind more quickly than I.

Then one day a few months before I was due to retire, I turned to the review section of one of the Sunday newspapers and there, to my amazement, was a photograph of Timothy.

I could hardly believe my eyes and wondered for an instant if it weren't merely a picture of some look-alike, but then there, underneath it I read the name, Timothy Hooper, followed by the words, "shades of Rupert Brooke?"

I looked back at the photograph. Although nearly five years had passed since I had last seen Timothy, stalking away from me across the frozen grass on that Sunday morning, and although he must now have been twenty-one years old, I still seemed to be looking at the face of a child. A dearly loved child. I imagined the green eyes and the red-gold hair and wondered what colour Rubert Brooke's hair had been. Still, I could see no physical resemblance between Rupert Brooke and Timothy except perhaps for the far-away romantic look in the eyes.

But then the comment about Rupert Brooke did not, of course, refer to Timothy's appearance, but rather to a slim volume of his poems which had only just been published. There was a short review.

I read it avidly. The poetry reflected, if not a mature innocence, an innocent maturity with a poetic vision of the world which was at once robust and romantic.

I read the review again. And again. It seemed then, and still does now, extraordinary that at so tender an age Timothy should actually have published a book of verse. I felt my heart swell with a strange mis-placed pride, almost as though this were an achievement of my own.

Then I looked again at the photograph of Timothy and I

remembered his anger on that Sunday morning, and I remembered all the intervening years of doubt and anxiety, and then I longed to see him, or just to hear his voice and then I put the paper down on my knee and closed my eyes and silently wept.

When I eventually collected myself, I decided that I must, at all costs, contact Timothy. However youthful he may have looked in his photograph, he was after all a grown-up now, and if he had not forgotten me, he must surely have forgiven me for whatever it was that he held against me.

So I sat down and wrote to him. I congratulated him on having his poems published, said that I was looking forward to buying them, told him how I had often thought of him over the years and how I had wondered what had become of him. I expressed a great desire to see him again, wished him well in the future and fervently hoped that if he had a moment he might find the time to drop me a line. I wanted to suggest that he came to see us all at Blenkinsop's, but remembering how unhappy he was there, not to mention the circumstances of his departure, I thought better of that.

I sent the letter to Timothy, care of his publisher.

I never saw Timothy again, or perhaps I should say that I have never yet seen him again. One day I may see him I suppose. But I did hear from him.

The letter came from France and reached me some four or five weeks after I had posted my own, by which time I was beginning to give up hope of ever receiving an answer. It was a nice letter and quite a long one. For days after it came I walked around the school unable to conceal my joy.

Timothy thanked me for writing, saying that he had been touched to hear from me. Touched. I was touched by that.

Blenkinsop's, he said, seemed to belong to another existence. He never thought of it now . . . anyway not if he could help it.

I supposed he never thought of me either. Why should he indeed?

He wondered if I had heard what had happened to him after he left. He had, he told me, gone to Paris where he and Natalie had lived a hand-to-mouth existence, washing up and waiting in restaurants, cleaning lavatories, walking dogs, minding children, cleaning offices and so forth. Then Natalie's father had paid for her to study art, so that now she earned a modest living as a commercial artist. They were still in France. But in a provincial town now. Timothy was writing a novel while earning his bread and butter playing a guitar in a small nightclub. Things had worked out very well for them. Timothy would recommend running away from school to anyone. It was the most sensible thing he had ever done.

With not a reference to the possibility of our ever meeting again, but I have to admit, a kindly reference to my cakes, Timothy thanked me again for my letter and signed off.

I later learned that Leo, on discovering Timothy's whereabouts, called on him and Natalie in France.

It is hardly surprising that he was not welcomed very warmly.

Natalie, Leo said, was frightful. Perfectly frightful. Not in the least bit friendly.

"Well I was hardly going to pounce on Timothy there and then," Leo shrieked dramatically.

"I should think not," I answered sharply. I wondered at Leo's audacity, and thought him silly to have gone raking up the past. I would certainly never think of calling unannounced on Timothy. Perhaps I am, as my name suggests, too prudent to invite the kind of rebuff which Leo experienced.

Leo felt sorry for Timothy, living as he did in one room with that odious girl. It couldn't last, he said.

I, on the other hand, felt relieved. For me and for Leo the whole episode should be over, closed, finished with. There was no further need for us to discuss it. Timothy was safe, apparently happy, successful and confident. What more could I ask for someone for whom I had cared so much.

Of course I would dearly love to see him again one day, but apart from that, it seemed to me then that there was nothing left for me to do but to mull over in my heart the events of those times and eventually to file them away in my memory for good. And this, I hope, is exactly what I have done by writing about the incident.

Now I must think of the future. But what, if anything does the future hold for me? I sigh and an autumnal melancholy descends on me once again.

*   *   *

Eric is back. For a day or two that is. He has left Morag in London and has come to pack up his house. It is under offer to a retired admiral. Eric hopes I will like him. I am not interested in the retired admiral.

But I am, of course, delighted to see Eric. More than delighted, but at the same time pained at the prospect of his leaving again.

He came to supper with me last night, looking, I thought, older and sadder.

The finality of the move clearly upsets him, besides which life in London does not entirely suit him. He feels too old for all that dirt and all the crowds and all the hustling and bustling and aggression and the petrol fumes and the traffic jams and the crime and the underground . . .

But Morag is different. Morag loves London. She has lived in cities all her life and cannot envisage spending more than a few days at a time in the country. She is younger than Eric and still enjoys the hurly-burly of the city. He sometimes wonders what he will do without a garden. Luckily the flat is close to the park.

Perhaps Morag will change her mind in a few years' time. You never know. Eric hopes that one day they'll come back to the country. Better not leave it too late or we'll all be dead.

I wonder to myself why on earth he is going away at all.

Eric looks at me and takes my hand.

"You probably wonder why I'm going," he says.

"It's none of my business what you do," I reply tartly.

He changes the conversation abruptly, drops my hand and says in an every day voice,

160

"Have you seen anything of Laurel lately? She hasn't been to London for a while. I wonder what she's up to."

Laurel has gone to a Polytechnic in the North of England to study comparative religions. I shall hear more about her on Sunday, no doubt, when I am due to have lunch with Victor and Patricia.

I am not looking forward to the occasion. Eric will have gone back to London by then so even without Patricia's traditional moaning, I shall be feeling rather gloomy. I have already gathered from speaking to her on the telephone that she is in her usual despondent state about both her children. I cannot think why, since one is away studying at a respectable college and the other is, at last, making a successful career for himself. But Patricia feels that this satisfactory state of affairs is hardly likely to last.

"Poor Laurel," says Eric. "She can be quite silly at times, but then can't we all?" He sighs.

"The truth is," he goes on, "that I have a weakness for Laurel."

I feel my heart contract.

"Not the kind of weakness you imagine, Prudence my dear. No. Not that. Not at all. It is just that my own daughter would have been exactly the same age and might have been, I suppose, just as silly."

I gasp.

"I'm so sorry," I say. "I had no idea . . ."

"How could you have known if I didn't tell you?" Then he clears his throat awkwardly and looks straight at me. "But I did tell you, if you remember, that Morag's daughter had died . . ."

Suddenly everything falls into place and I feel tremendous compassion for Eric, and an overwhelming sadness.

Eric does not like to talk about himself but, for some reason, he feels that he owes me an explanation. After all I have been a good friend to him over the past year, he says, and we have had some happy times.

Eric's liaison with Morag lasted for years. Because of the child it dragged on long after it should have died a natural death. When the child died they became united in grief and grew closer to each other again. Eric's wife, who was a good woman, never knew about the child, never even knew about Morag, he thinks, but you can't be sure.

Many years ago Eric and Morag agreed that if they were ever to find themselves alone, they would settle down together. He still feels bound by this agreement because Morag is so very, very lonely and because he has been the cause of so much suffering in her life. Of course he is fond of Morag. Very fond indeed. He is sure that he is making the right decision and that it will all be for the best in the end.

But at the moment he is tired and sad at having to leave his home and the countryside.

"I'm exhausted," he says and pats my knee. "I must go back to bed. I expect I'll feel better in the morning."

As Eric left me last night he looked like an old, old man. Old and world-weary.

This morning I was up early, having slept rather badly, and have been sitting writing my diary at my kitchen table since seven o'clock. I must try to put on a cheerful face for Eric's sake today as I have promised to go round and see him this afternoon for a last cup of tea in his house and to prevent him from being too gloomy. It is always sad to see the contents of a house packed up. Tomorrow he goes back to London.

October 19th

Just before I left home to go and see Eric yesterday afternoon Patricia rang. She was in a dreadful state and wanted me to come round and see her immediately. I told her firmly that I was coming to lunch on Sunday but simply could not manage to get over before then.

"But Prudence," she wailed, "It's the children . . . and Victor . . . I don't know what to do about Victor . . . or the children . . ."

If I had not been so concerned for Eric and so sad at having to wish him farewell, I would have been tempted to laugh at what Patricia told me next.

Laurel, in her studies of comparative religions, has come across

Tantric Buddhism which she has decided to espouse as the one true faith. Tantrism, according to Laurel — Patricia thinks she must have made some mistake — centres around the idea that divine bliss, wisdom and peace of mind can only be achieved through the sexual act. With this in mind Laurel has set about desperately and frantically seeking this divine bliss at every opportunity.

Whenever she comes home she lectures her parents ceaselessly about her search and urgently beseeches them to embrace the same ideal.

Victor is so disgusted by what his daughter has to say that he has bought a pair of ear-plugs which he solemnly puts in his ears whenever Laurel is in the house.

And, as if all that weren't enough to drive anyone to distraction, Victor has forbidden Leo to cross his threshold, for Leo — Patricia is in tears now — has come right out of his closet and my ridiculous pusillanimous brother is frightened of catching AIDS from his own son. Patricia is weeping for the grandchildren she will never have.

I despair of Victor and Patricia, but nevertheless I promise to come early on Sunday and to have a word with Victor.

"Tell him to take his ear-plugs out before I come," I told Patricia sharply.

Despite my mood as I put the telephone down, I couldn't help smiling to myself at the thought of Victor and Patricia adopting Tantrism.

When I eventually arrived at Eric's house in time for a cup of tea, I went round to the back and as I pushed open the door and stepped into the kitchen I was surprised to hear Eric singing. He was boiling a kettle and he looked much more relaxed than he did the night before.

> "Wait 'til the sun shines Nellie
> Don't you cry,
> We will be happy Nellie,
> By and by . . ." he sang.

"How nice to hear you singing," I said.

"I used to do it rather well," he replied, unusually boastful. "But I'm afraid the old voice is a bit off key nowadays."

Then he looked at me with a funny smile and said,

"Prudence, I've changed my mind. I'm not going. I'm too old for such an upheaval. I've spoken to Morag this morning. She feels the same. And I've taken the house off the market — it's too bad about the admiral ... I've spent all morning unpacking everything I packed yesterday ..."

I began to laugh ... and to laugh ... and to laugh.

"What on earth are you laughing at?" Eric asked me with a startled look.

"It's just Laurel," I spluttered. "She's become a Tantric Buddhist ... and Leo's come out of his closet at last ... poor, dear Patricia ..."